D0975780

Dear parents, caregivers, and educators:

If you want to get your child excited about reading, you've come to the right place! Ready-to-Read *GRAPHICS* is the perfect launchpad for emerging graphic novel readers.

All Ready-to-Read *GRAPHICS* books include the following:

- ★ **A how-to guide to reading graphic novels for first-time readers**

- ★ **Easy-to-follow panels to support reading comprehension**

- ★ **Accessible vocabulary to build your child's reading confidence**

- ★ **Compelling stories that star your child's favorite characters**

- ★ **Fresh, engaging illustrations that provide context and promote visual literacy**

Wherever your child may be on their reading journey, Ready-to-Read *GRAPHICS* will make them giggle, gasp, and want to keep reading more.

Blast off on this starry adventure . . . a universe of graphic novel reading awaits!

Esbaum, Jill,
Friends do not eat
friends /
2021.
33305251910240
sa   07/12/21

THUNDER AND CLUCK

Friends **Do Not** Eat Friends

For Bria & Will
—J. E.

Thanks to Warren
for all of those drawing lessons
—M. T.

SIMON SPOTLIGHT
An imprint of Simon & Schuster Children's Publishing Division
1230 Avenue of the Americas, New York, New York 10020
This Simon Spotlight edition June 2021
Text copyright © 2021 by Jill Esbaum
Illustrations copyright © 2021 by Christopher M. Thompson
All rights reserved, including the right of reproduction in whole or in part in any form.
SIMON SPOTLIGHT, READY-TO-READ, and colophon are registered trademarks
of Simon & Schuster, Inc. For information about special discounts for bulk
purchases, please contact Simon & Schuster Special Sales at 1-866-506-1949 or
business@simonandschuster.com.
Manufactured in the United States of America 0521 LAK
10 9 8 7 6 5 4 3 2 1
Library of Congress Cataloging-in-Publication Data
Names: Esbaum, Jill, author. | Thompson, Miles (Illustrator) illustrator. | Title: Friends do
not eat friends / by Jill Esbaum ; illustrated by Miles Thompson. | Description: New York,
New York : Simon Spotlight, 2021. | Series: Thunder & Cluck | Audience: Ages 4–6. |
Summary: Big, scary, and hungry Thunder the dinosaur wants to chase and chomp Cluck, a
small but brave dinosaur, but Cluck has decided that they will be friends. | Identifiers: LCCN
2020036051 | ISBN 9781534486515 (paperback) | ISBN 9781534486522 (hardcover)
| ISBN 9781534486539 (ebook) | Subjects: CYAC: Dinosaurs—Fiction. | Friendship—
Fiction. | Classification: LCC PZ7.E74458 Ft 2021 | DDC [E—dc23] | LC record available
at https://lccn.loc.gov/2020036051

THUNDER AND CLUCK

Friends Do Not Eat Friends

Written by **JILL ESBAUM**
Illustrated by **MILES THOMPSON**

Ready-to-Read *GRAPHICS*

Simon Spotlight
New York   London   Toronto   Sydney   New Delhi

HOW TO READ THIS BOOK

THUNDER and CLUCK are here to give you some tips on reading this book.

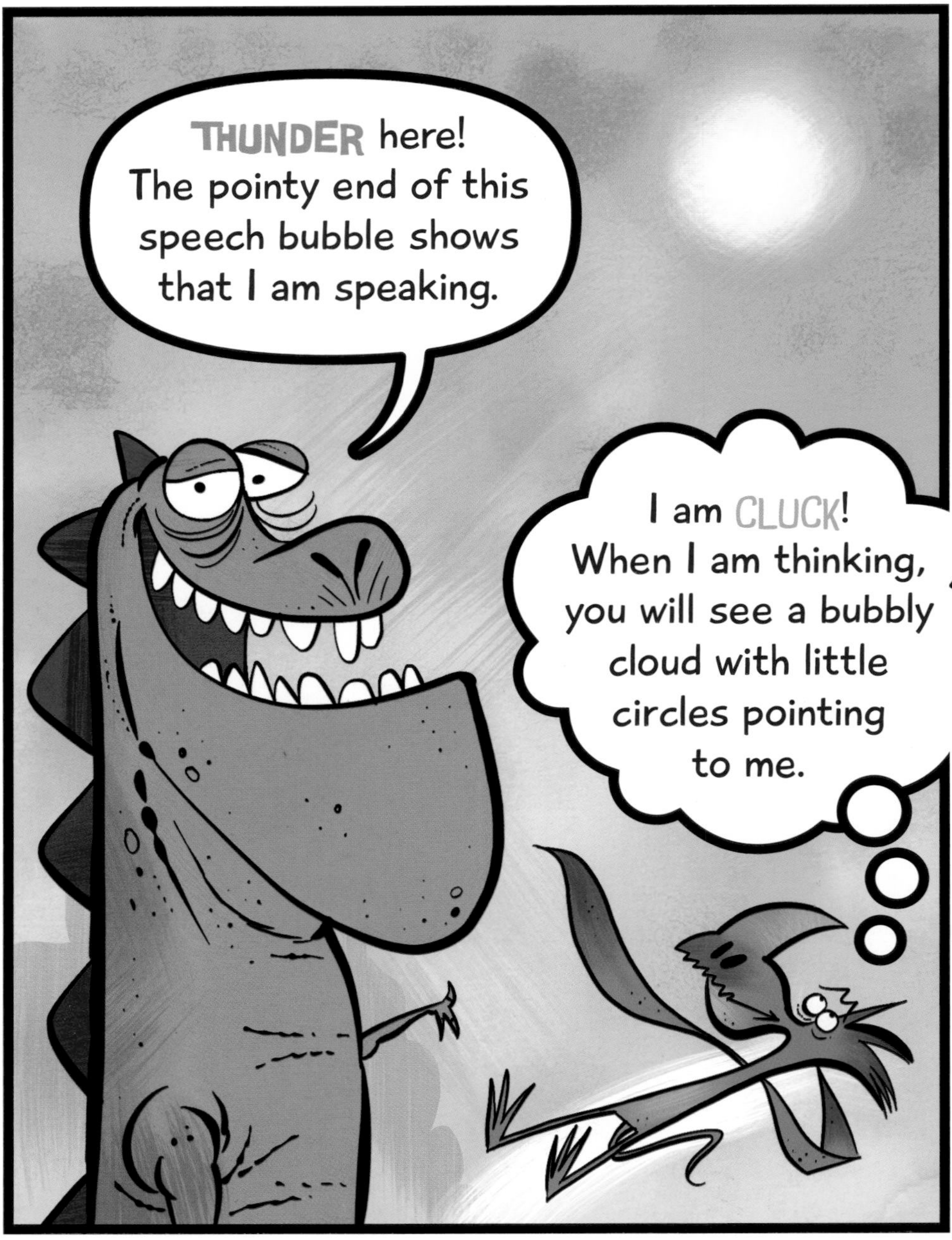
THUNDER here! The pointy end of this speech bubble shows that I am speaking.
I am CLUCK! When I am thinking, you will see a bubbly cloud with little circles pointing to me.

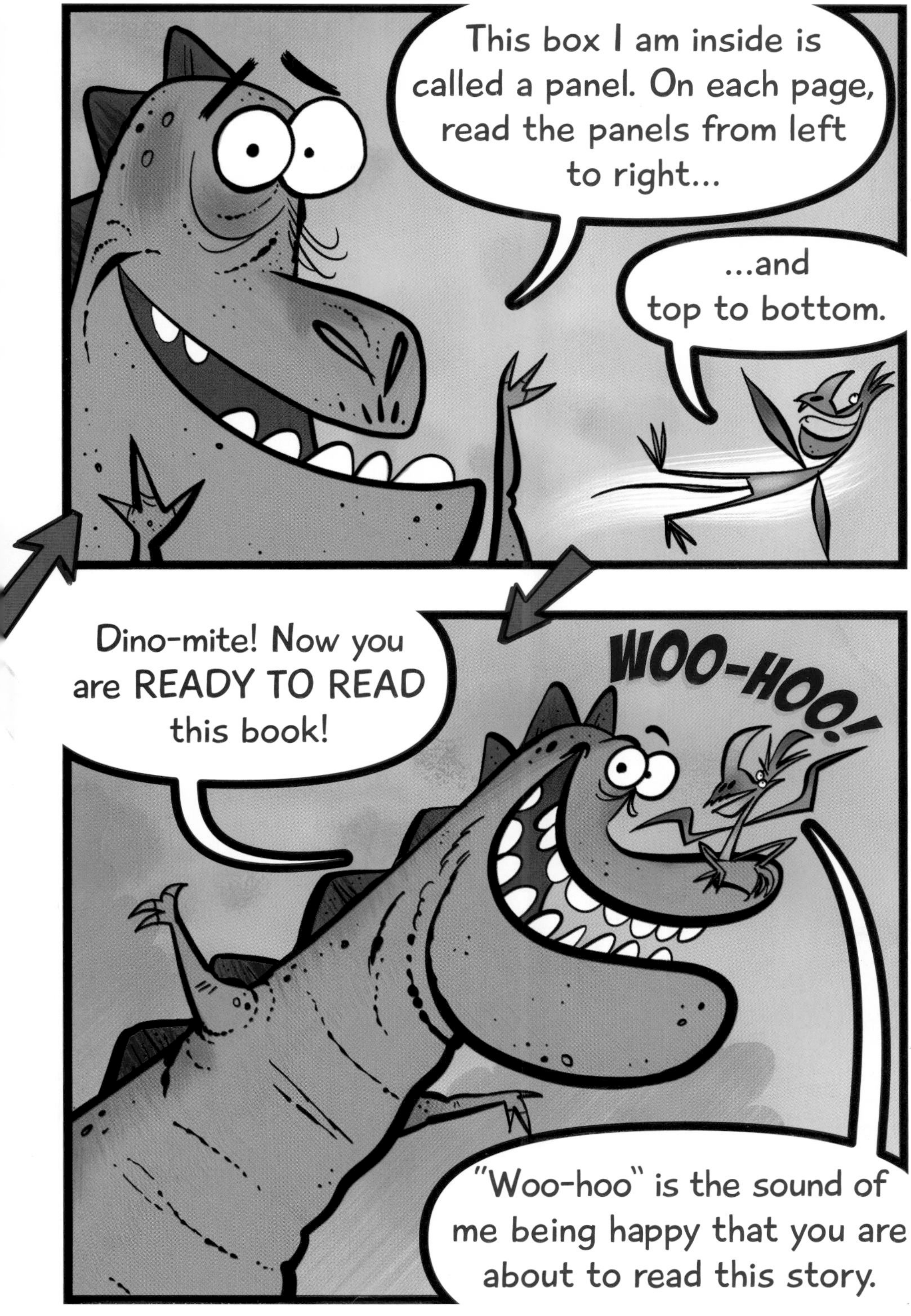
This box I am inside is called a panel. On each page, read the panels from left to right...
...and top to bottom.
Dino-mite! Now you are READY TO READ this book!
WOO-HOO!
"Woo-hoo" is the sound of me being happy that you are about to read this story.

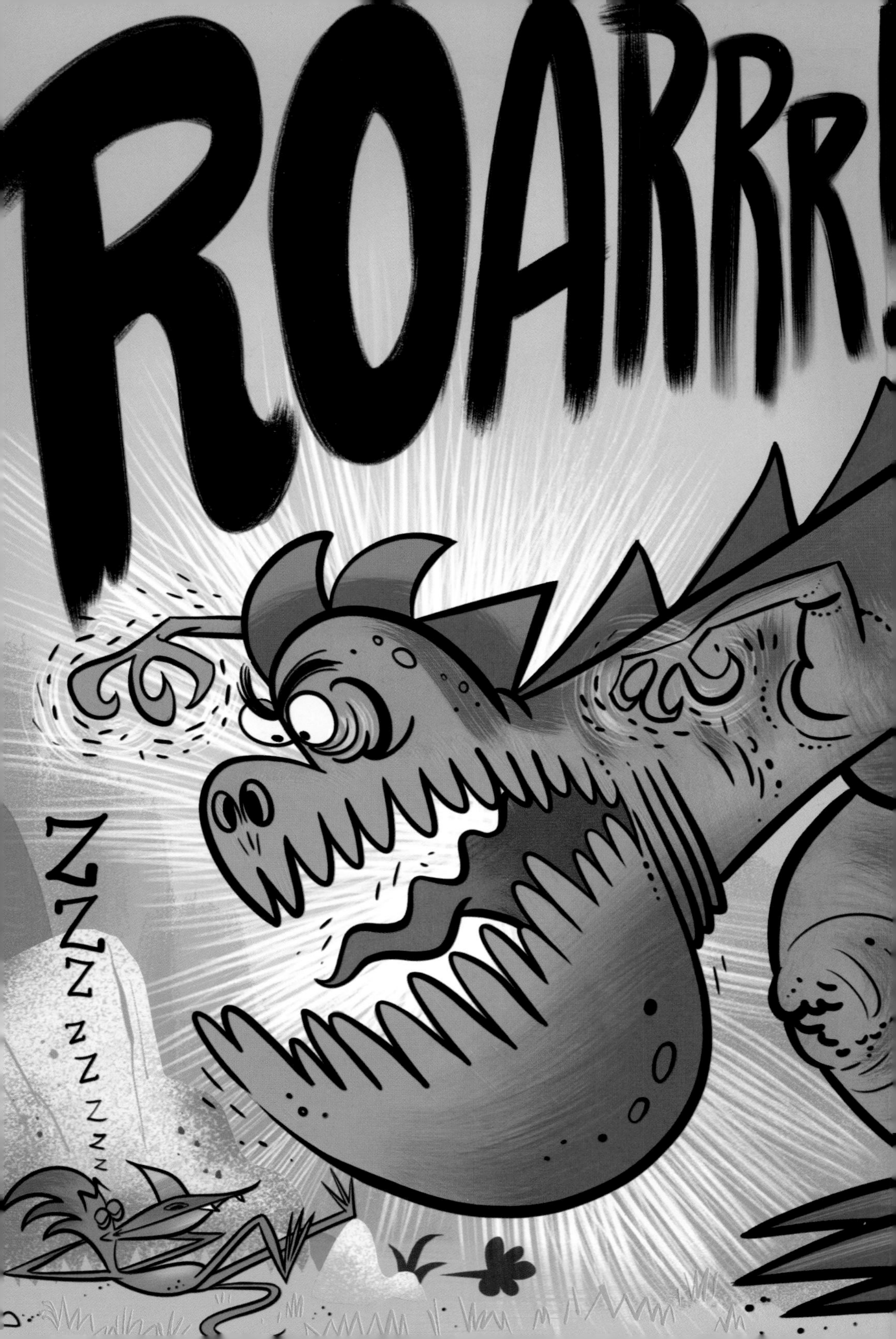
ROARRR!
ZZZZZZZZZZ

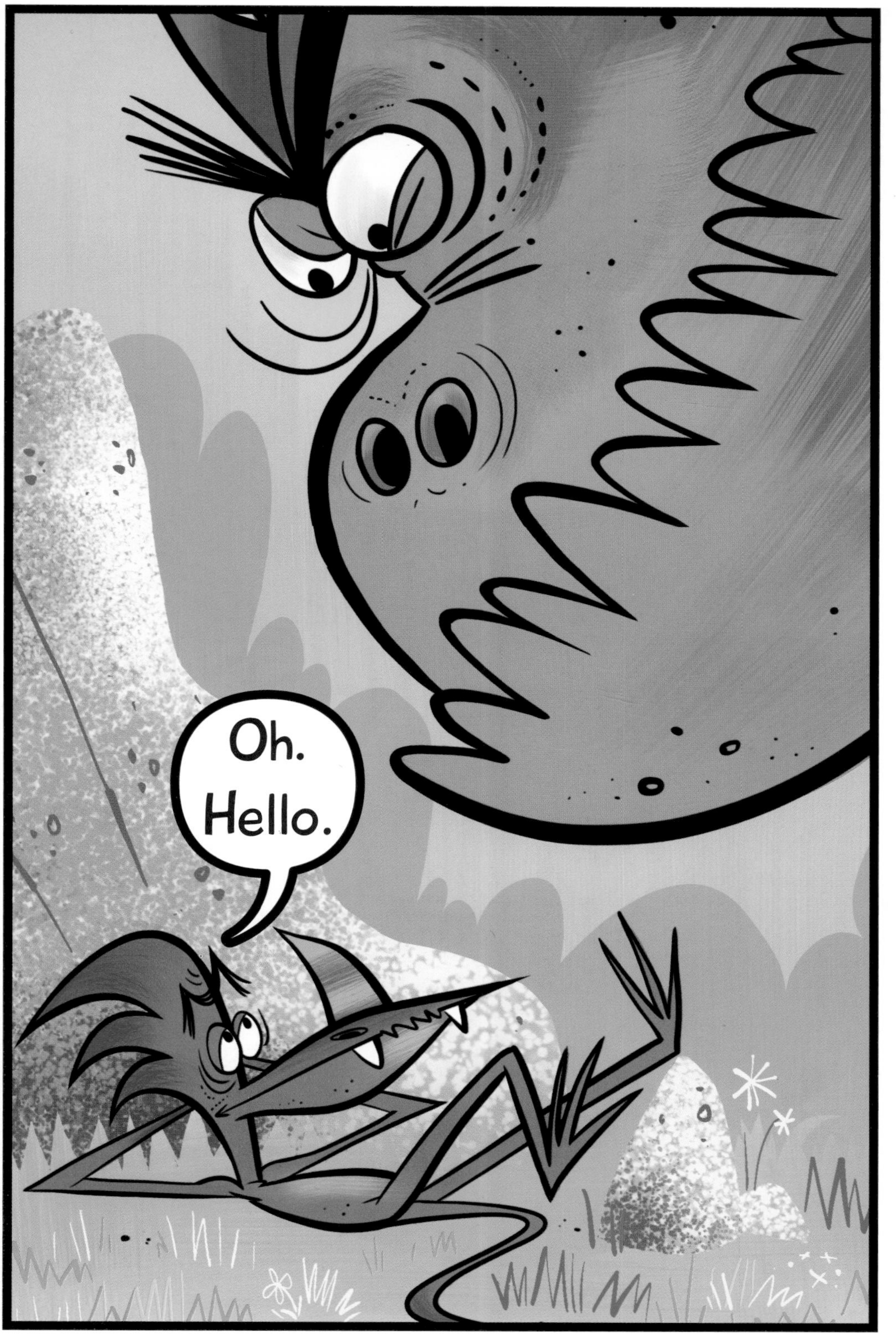
Oh. Hello.

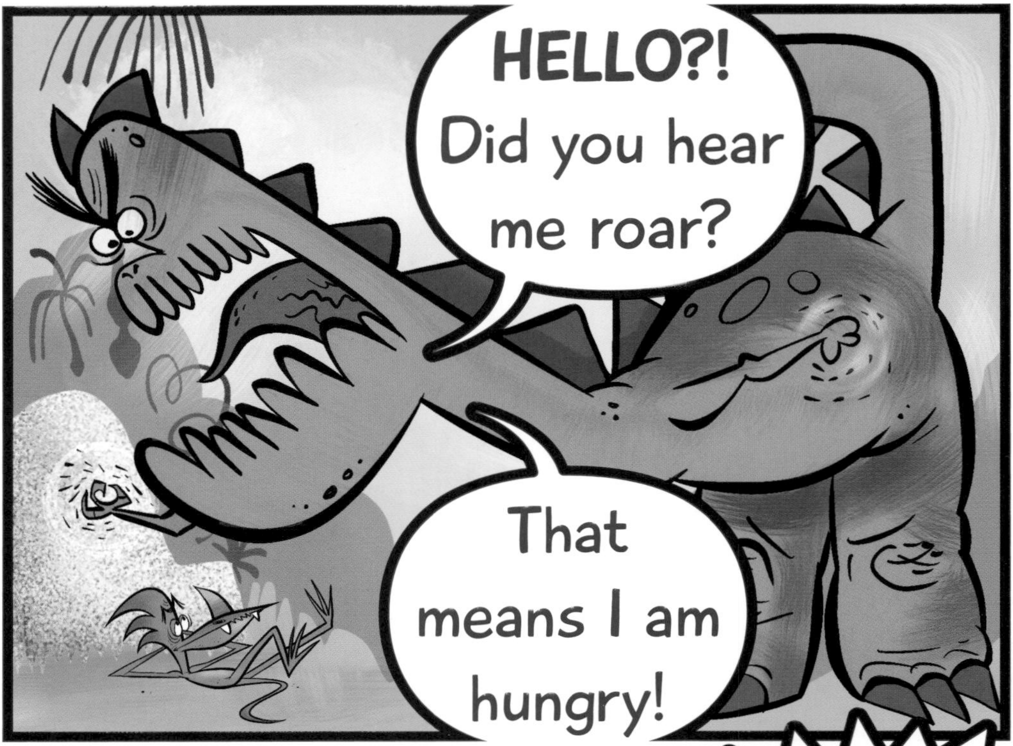
HELLO?! Did you hear me roar?
That means I am hungry!

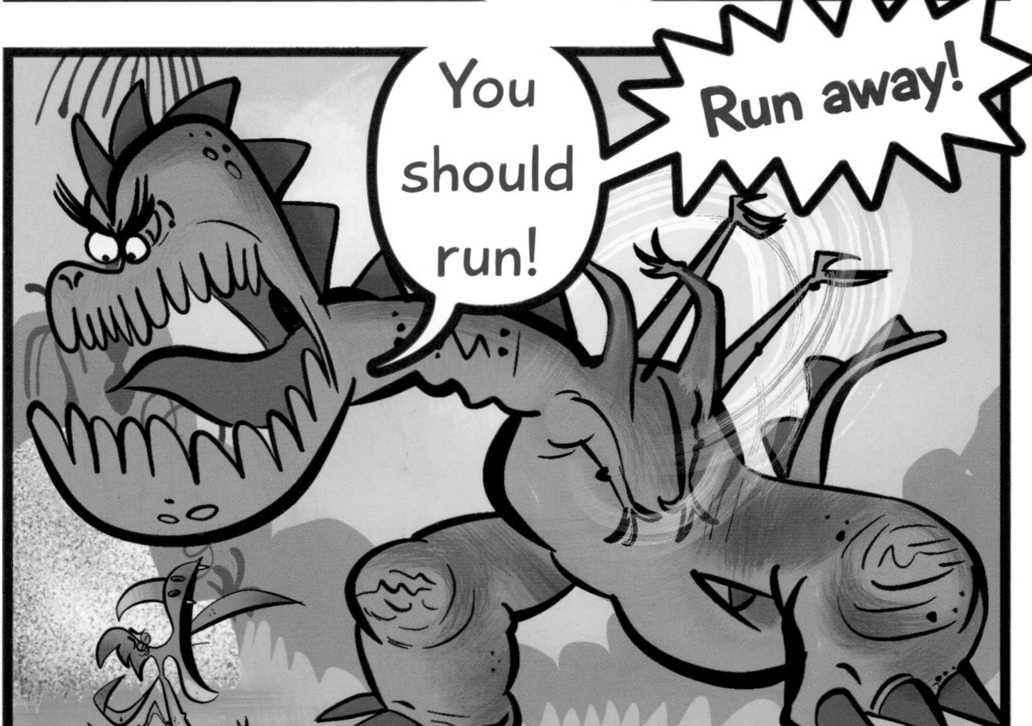
You should run!
Run away!

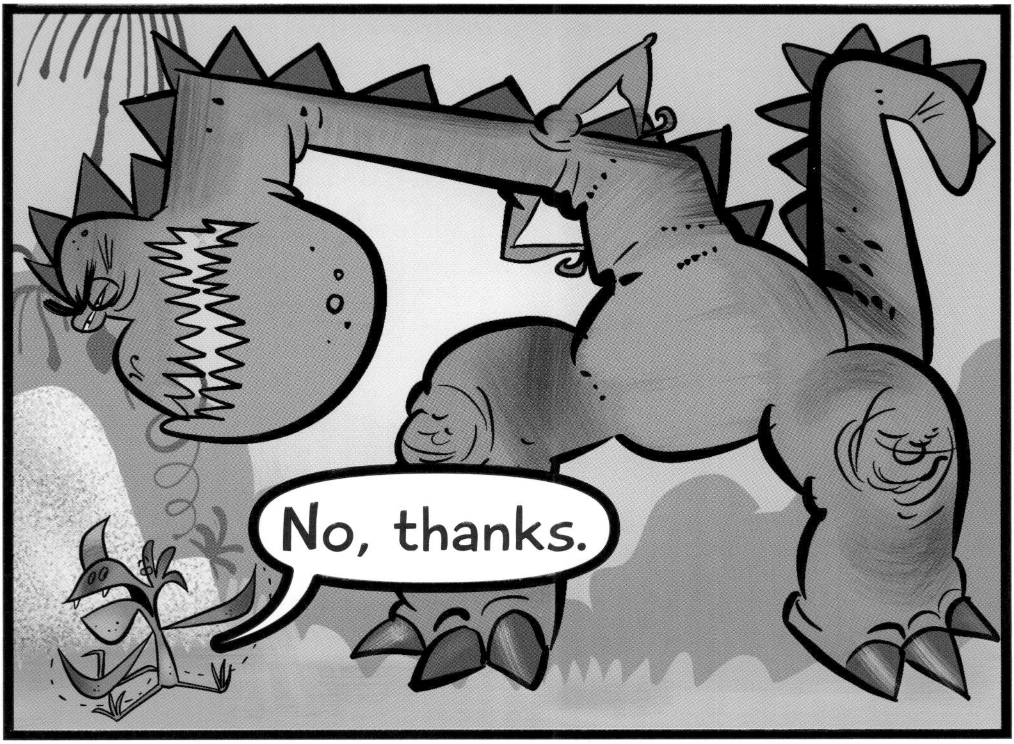
No, thanks.

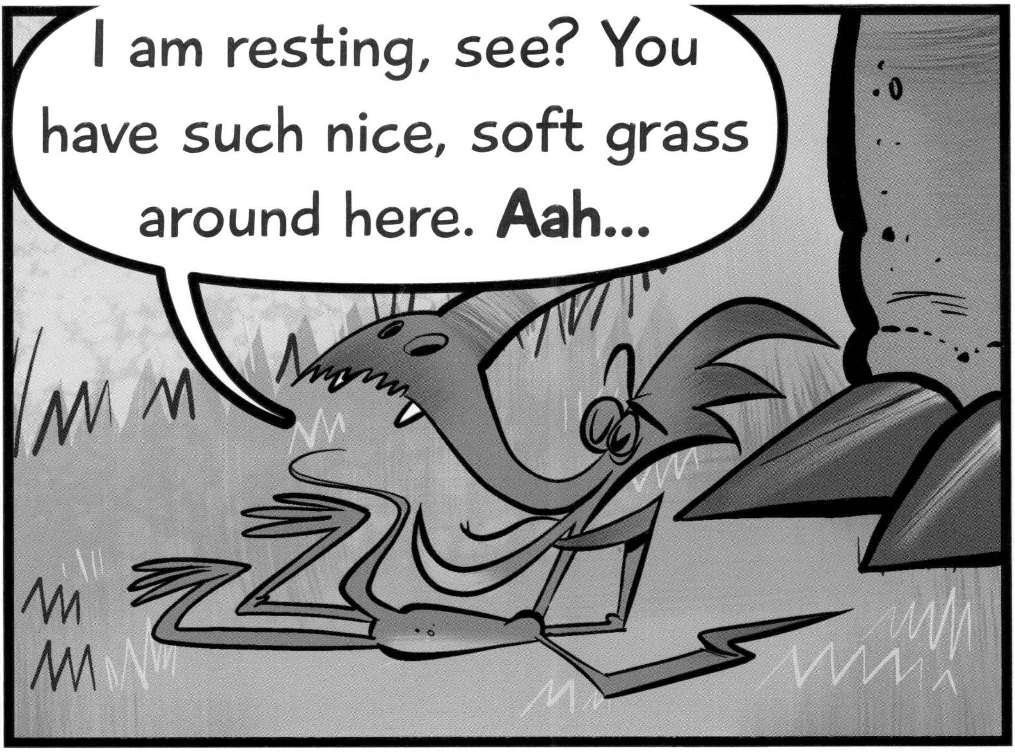
I am resting, see? You have such nice, soft grass around here. **Aah...**

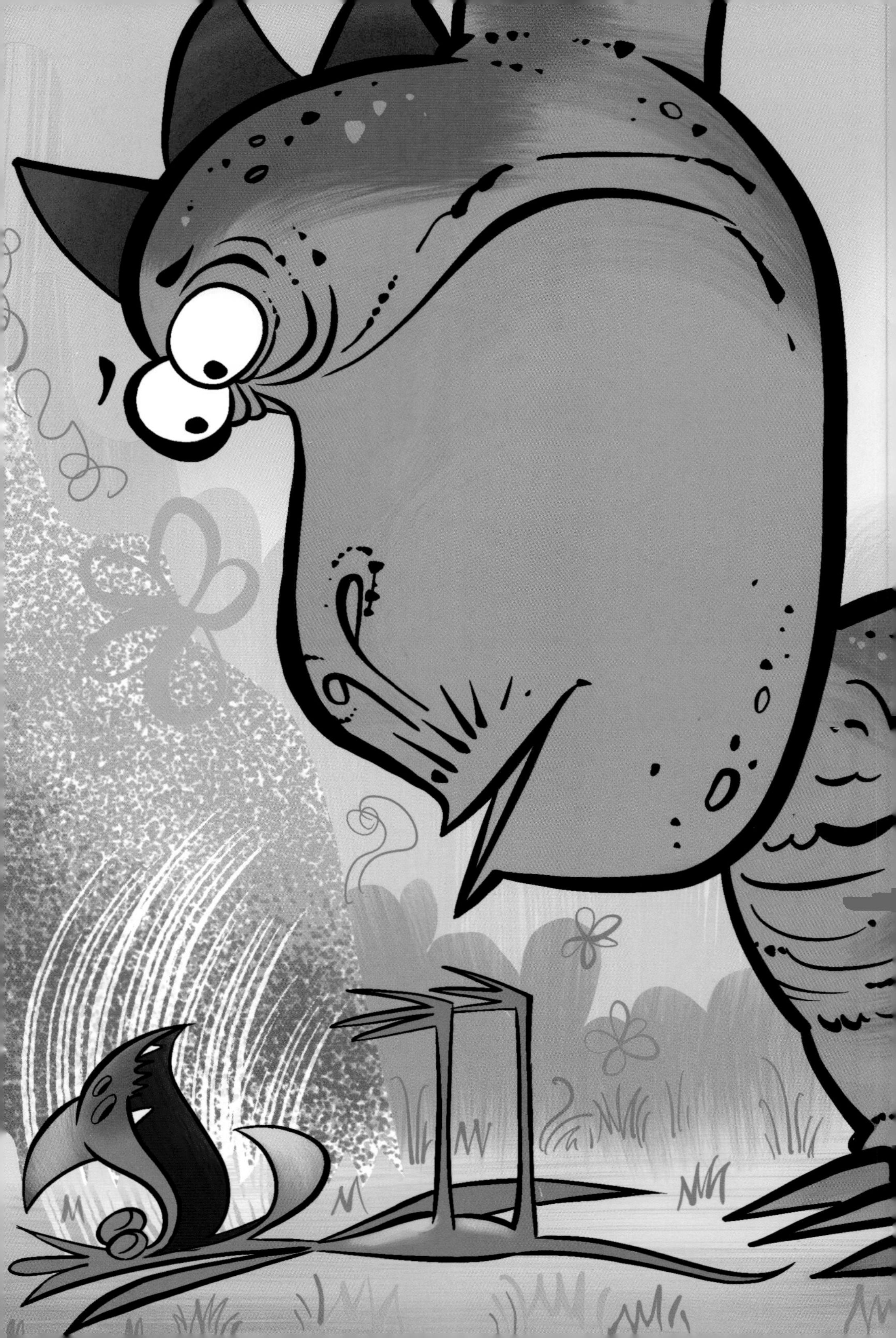

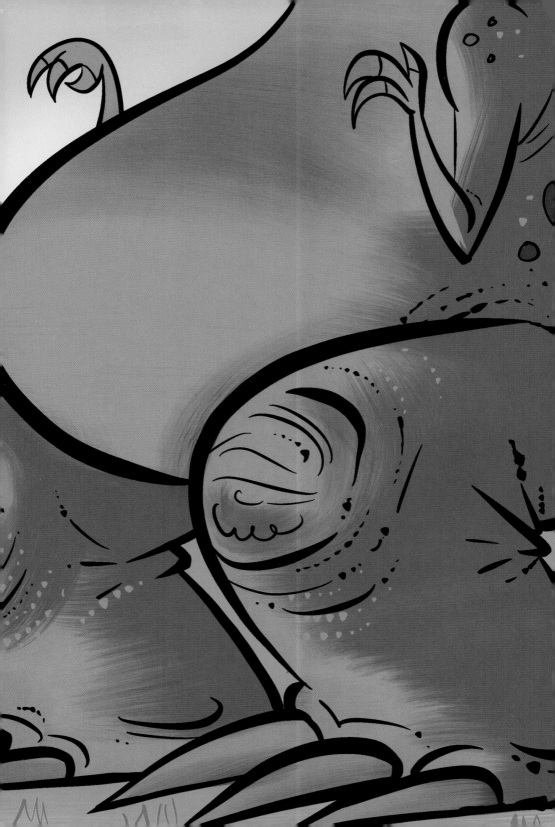

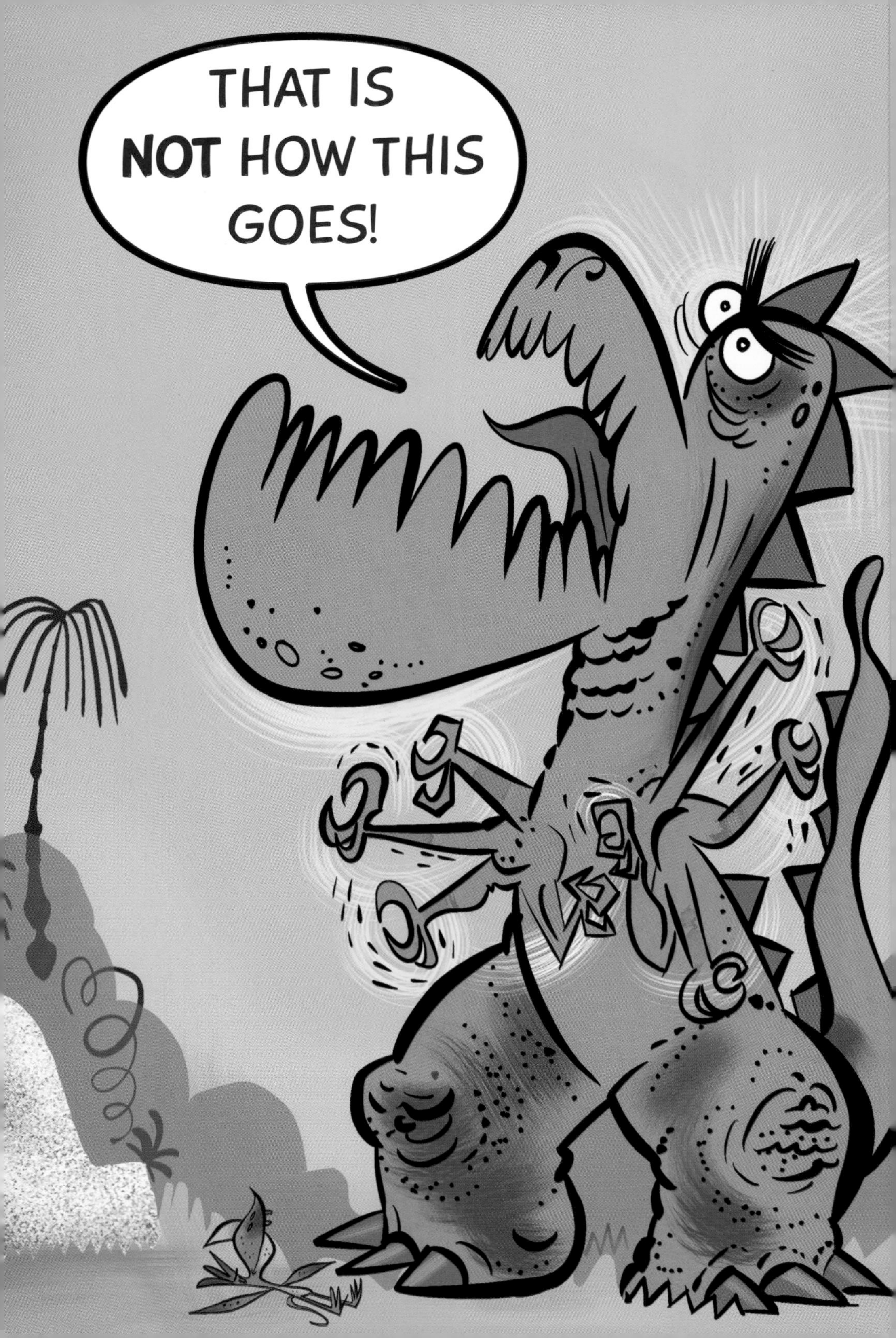
THAT IS NOT HOW THIS GOES!

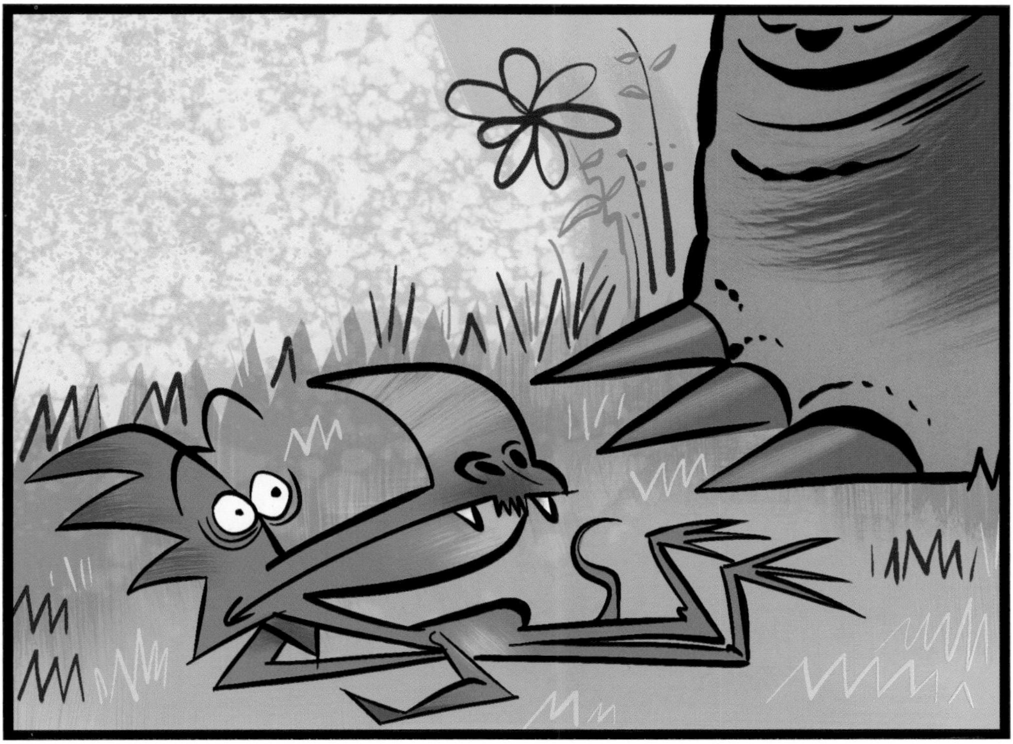

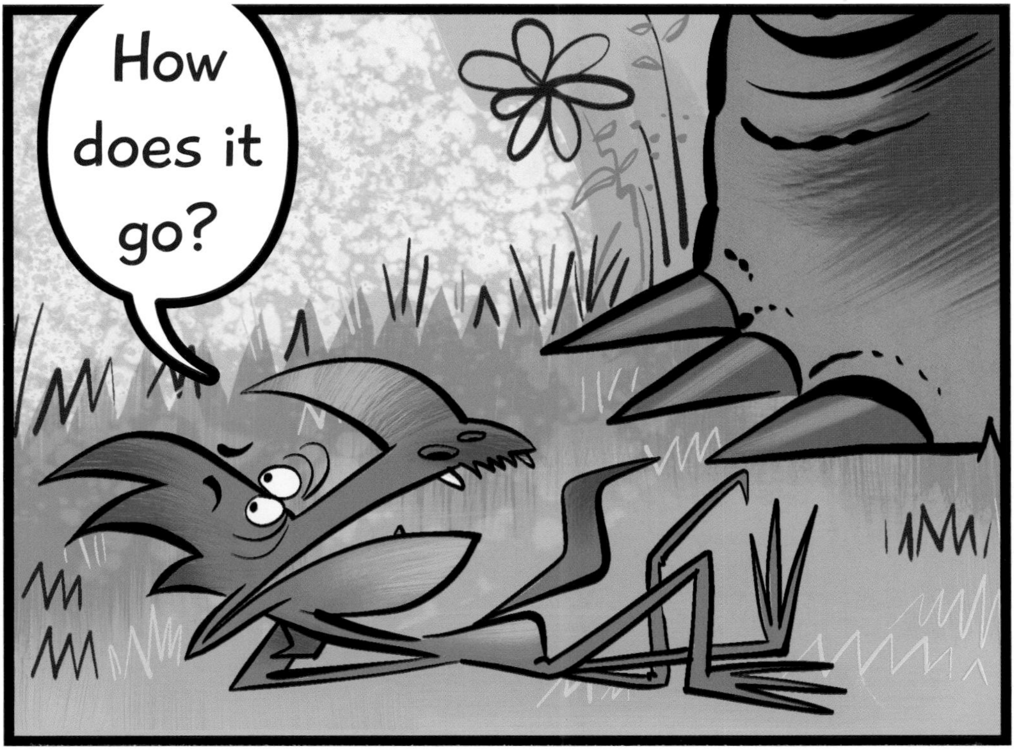
How does it go?

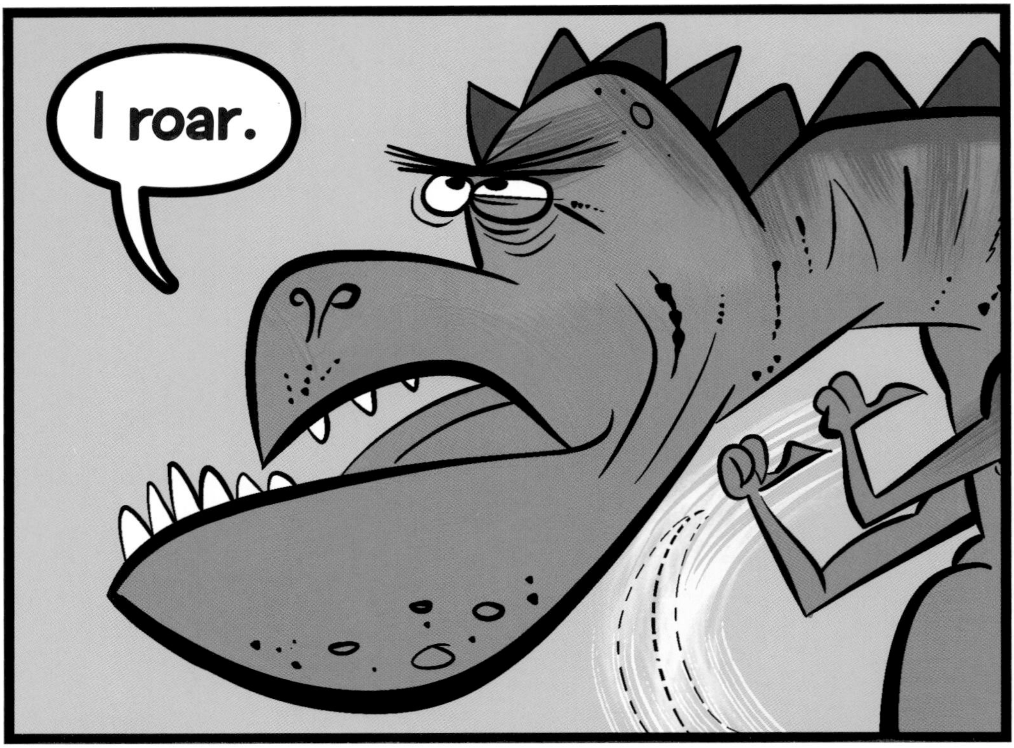
I roar.

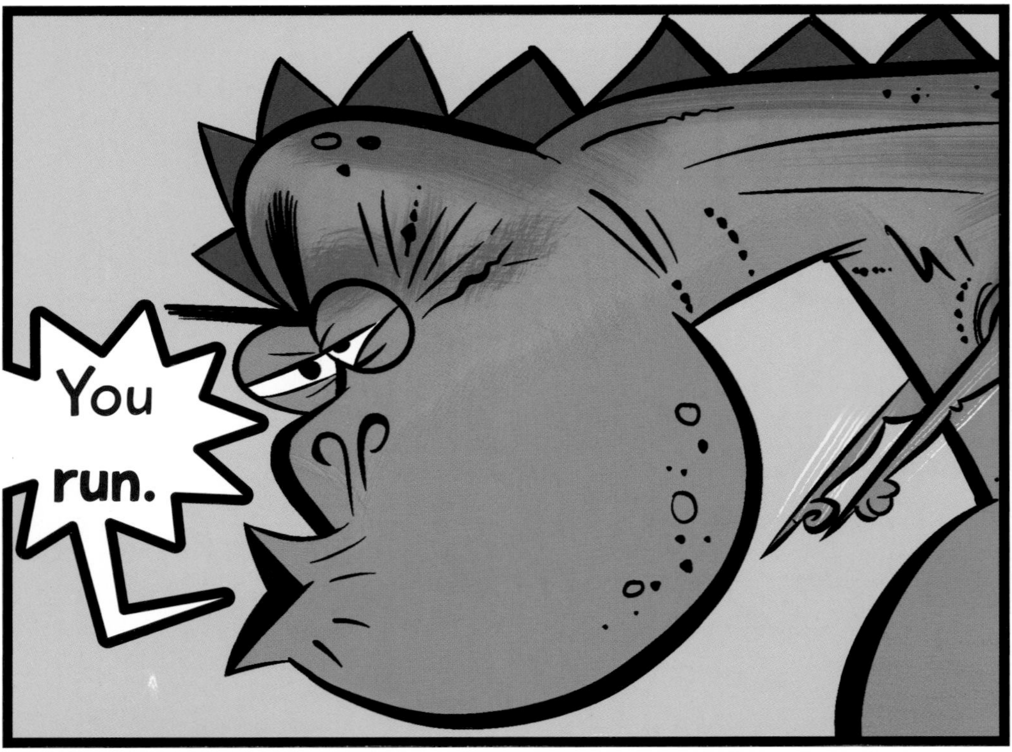
You run.

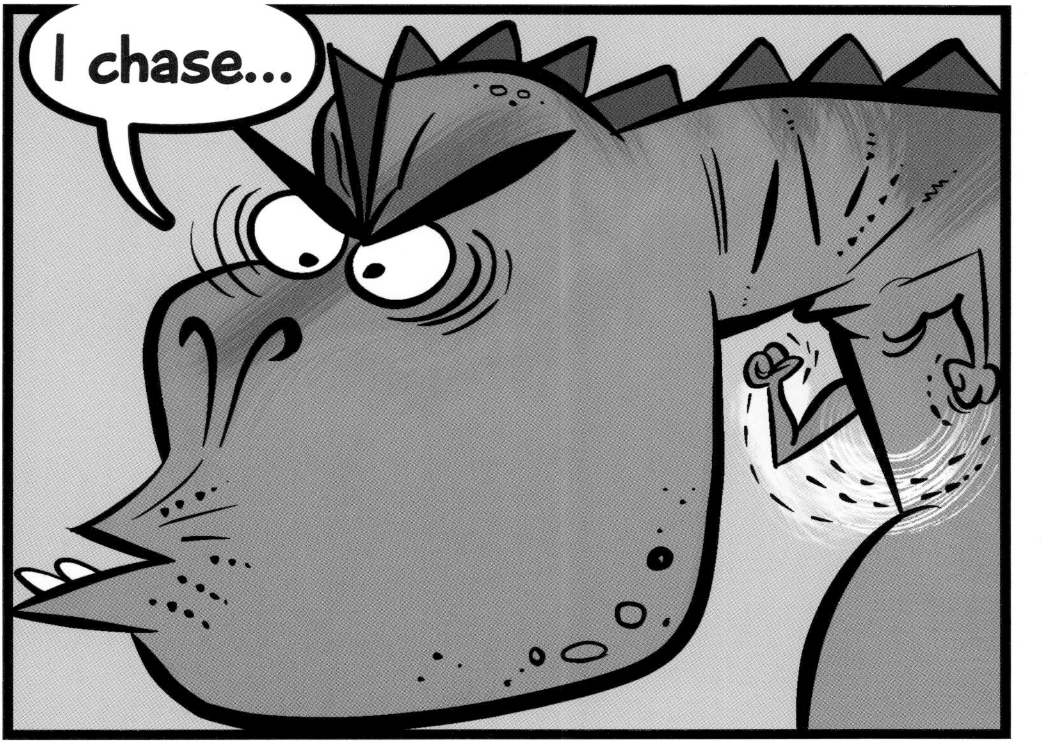
I chase...

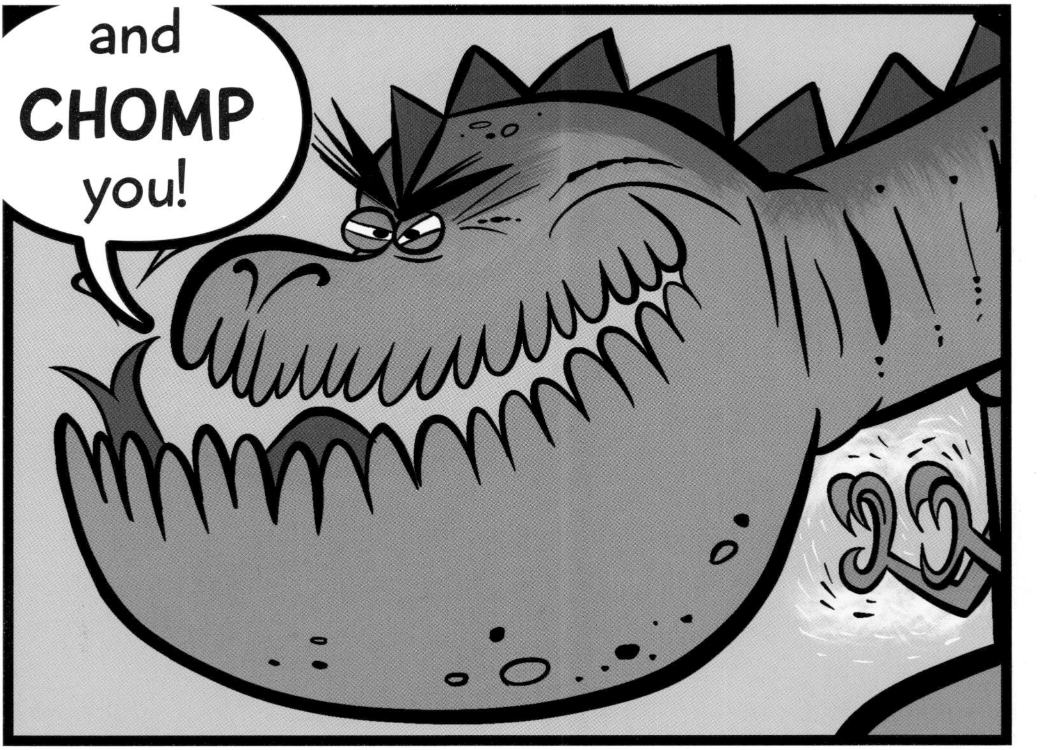
and **CHOMP** you!

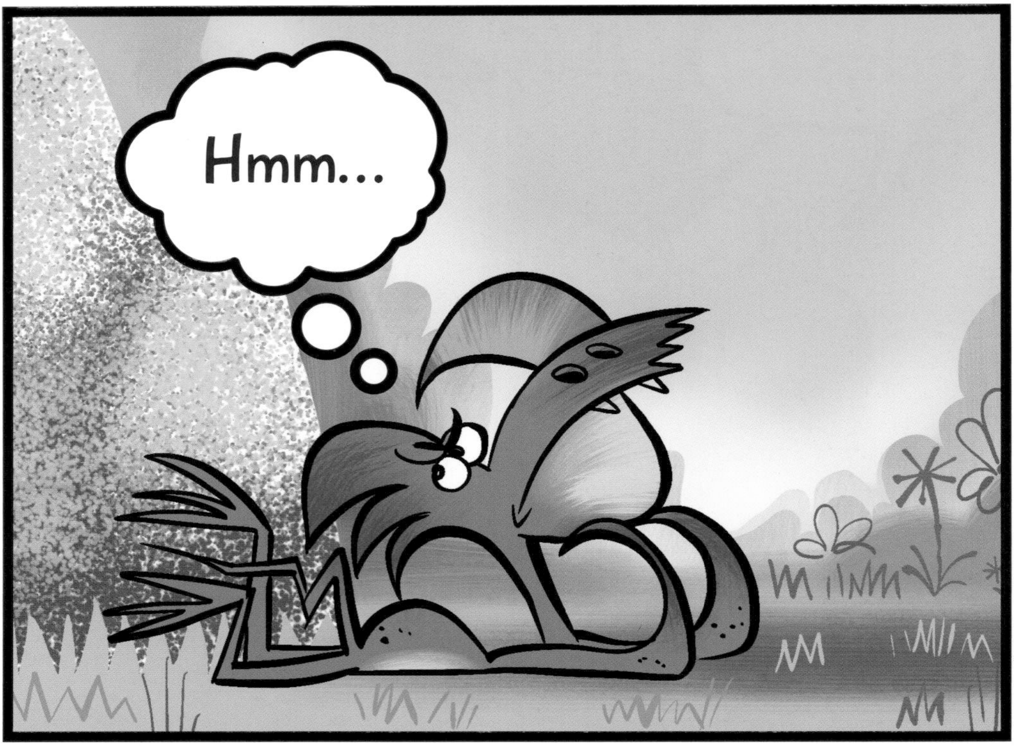
Hmm...

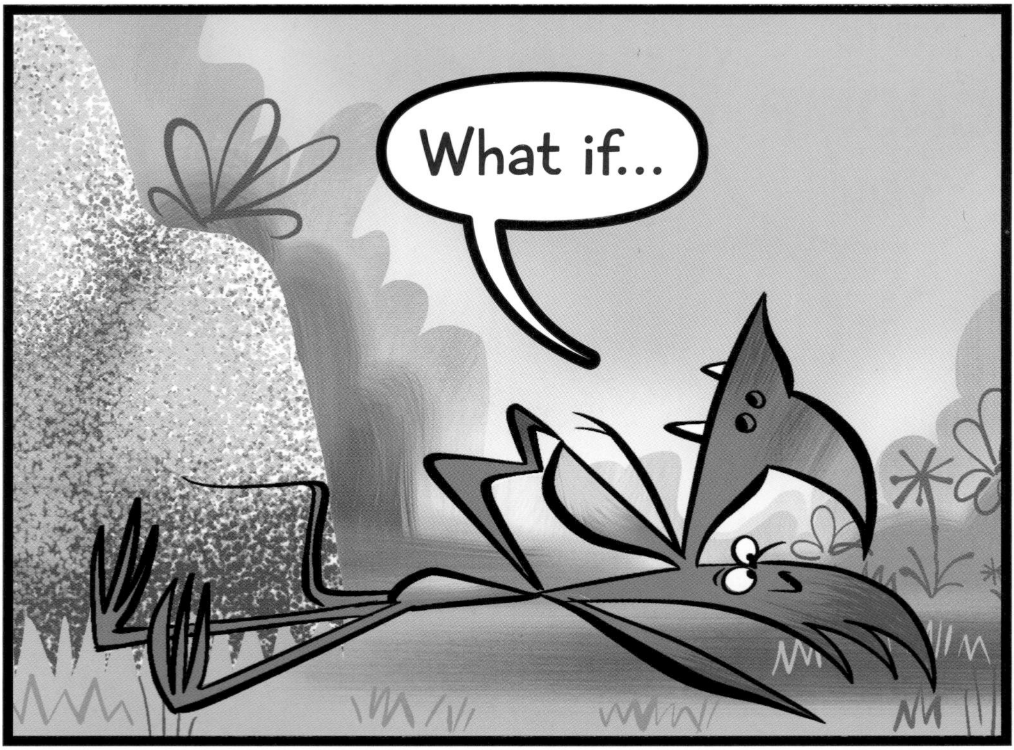
What if...

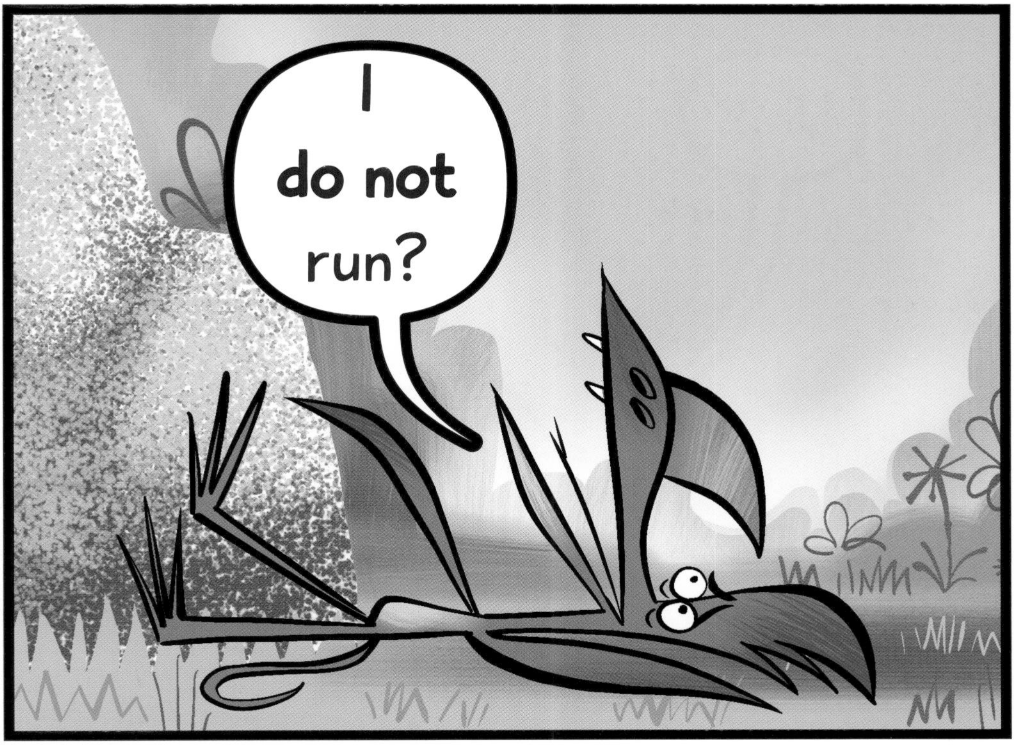
I do not run?

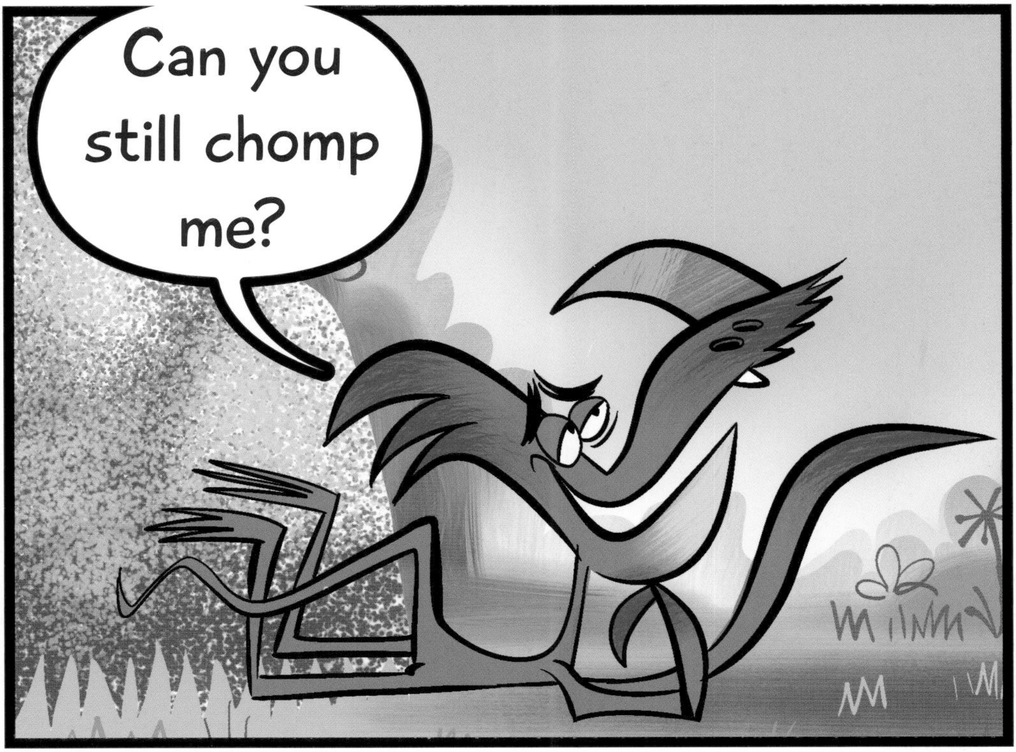
Can you still chomp me?

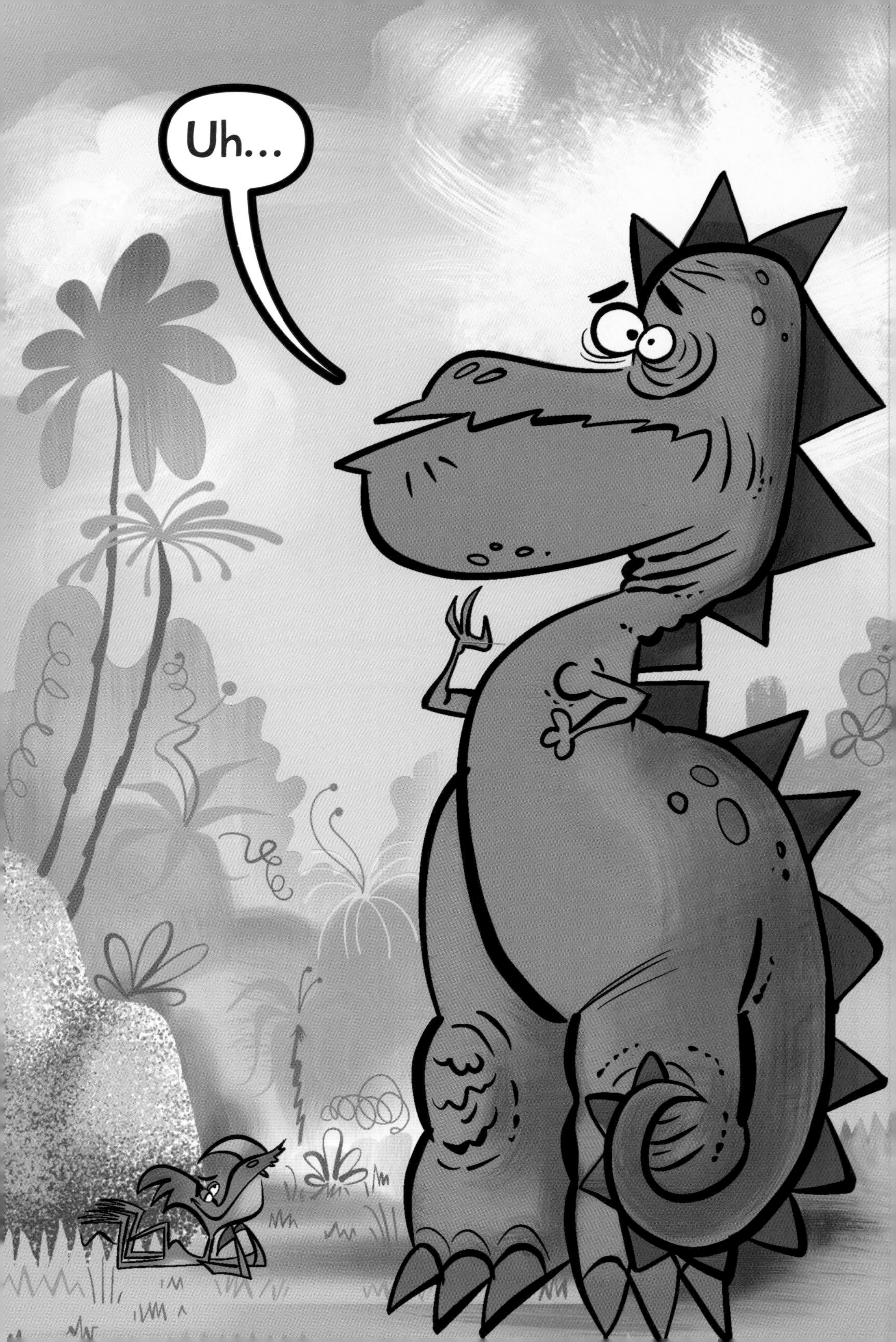
Uh...

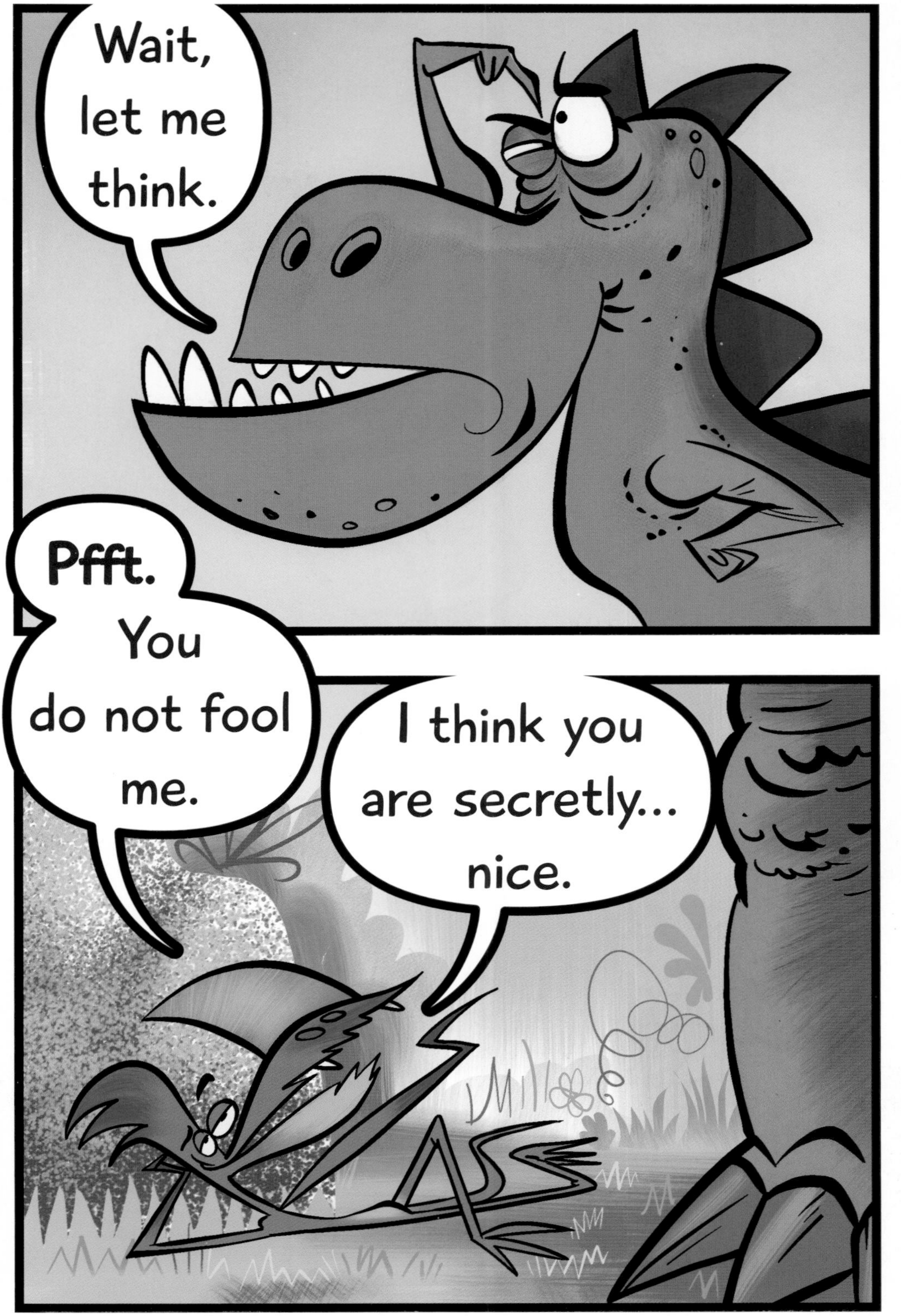
Wait, let me think.
Pfft. You do not fool me.
I think you are secretly... nice.

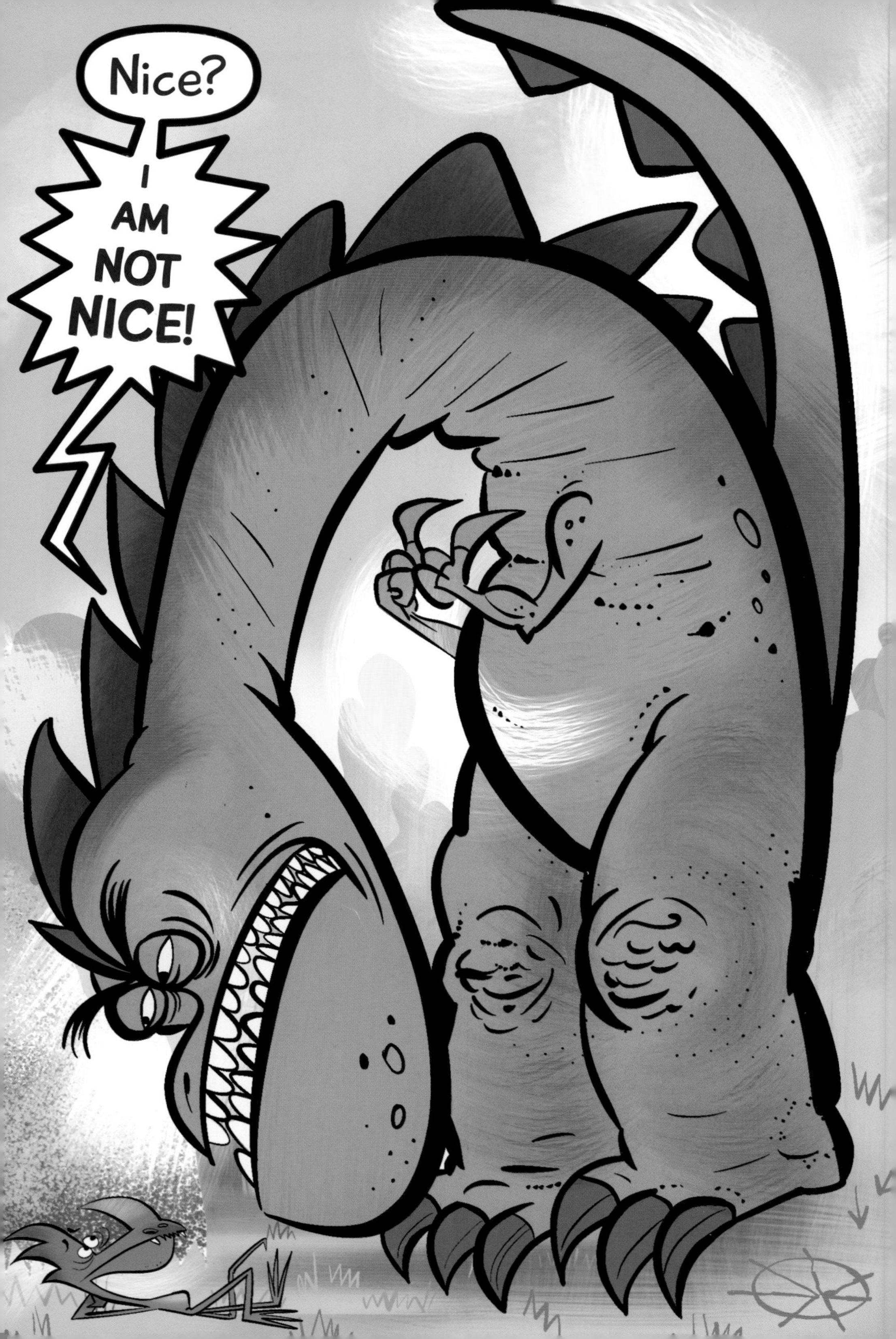
Nice?
I AM NOT NICE!

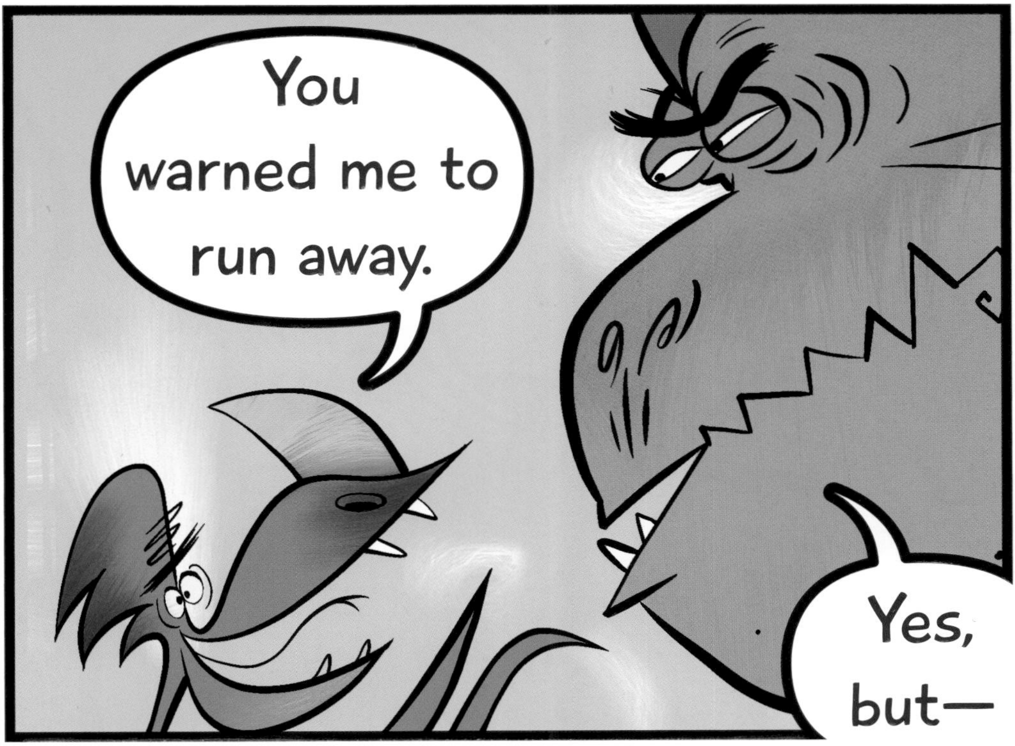
You warned me to run away.
Yes, but—

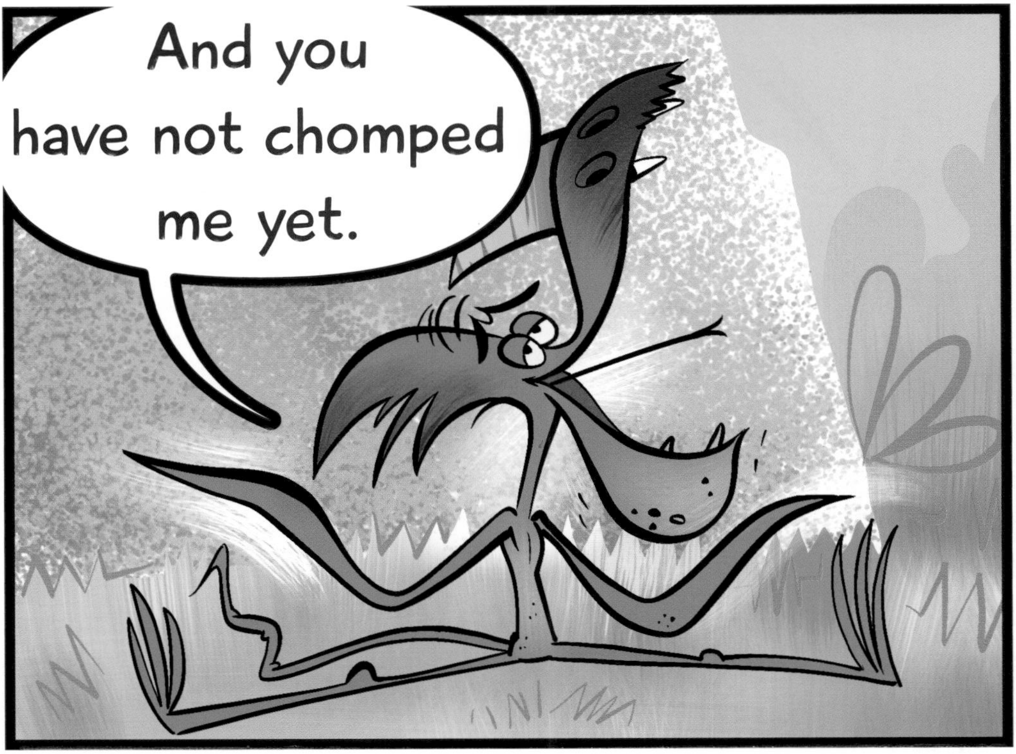
And you have not chomped me yet.

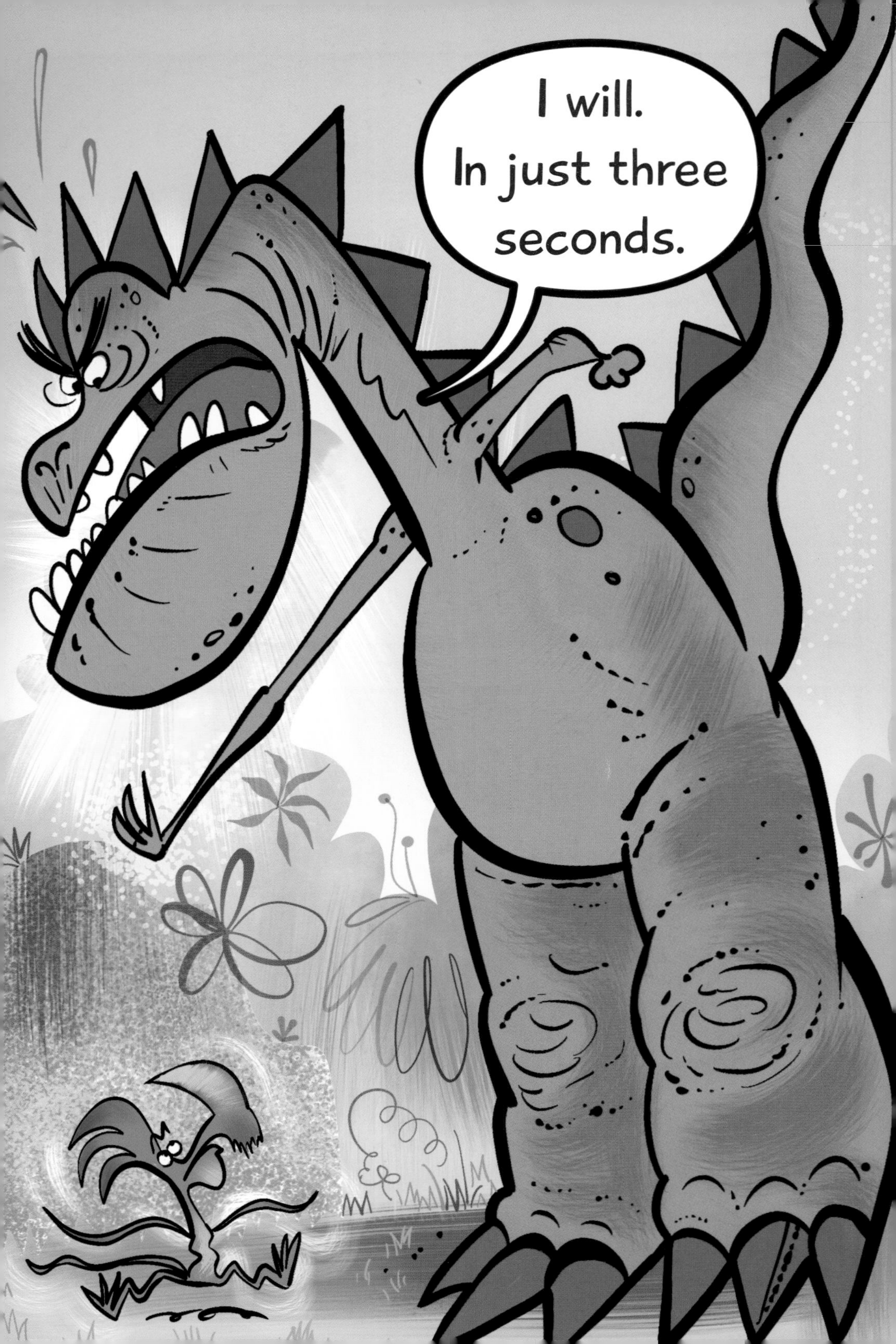
I will. In just three seconds.

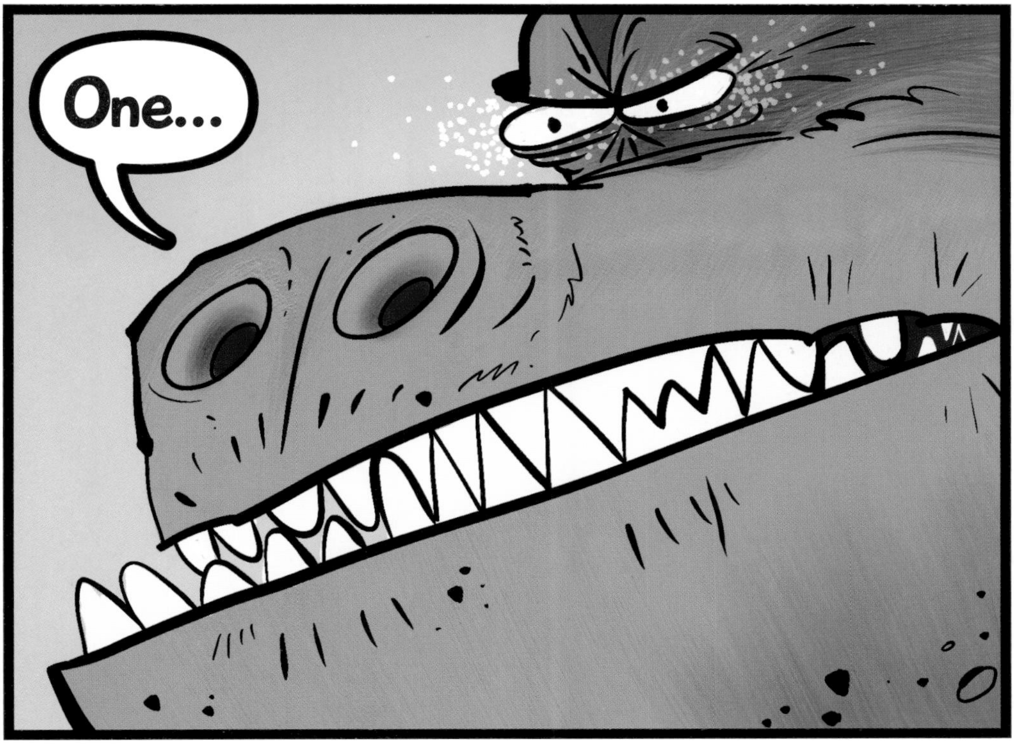
One...

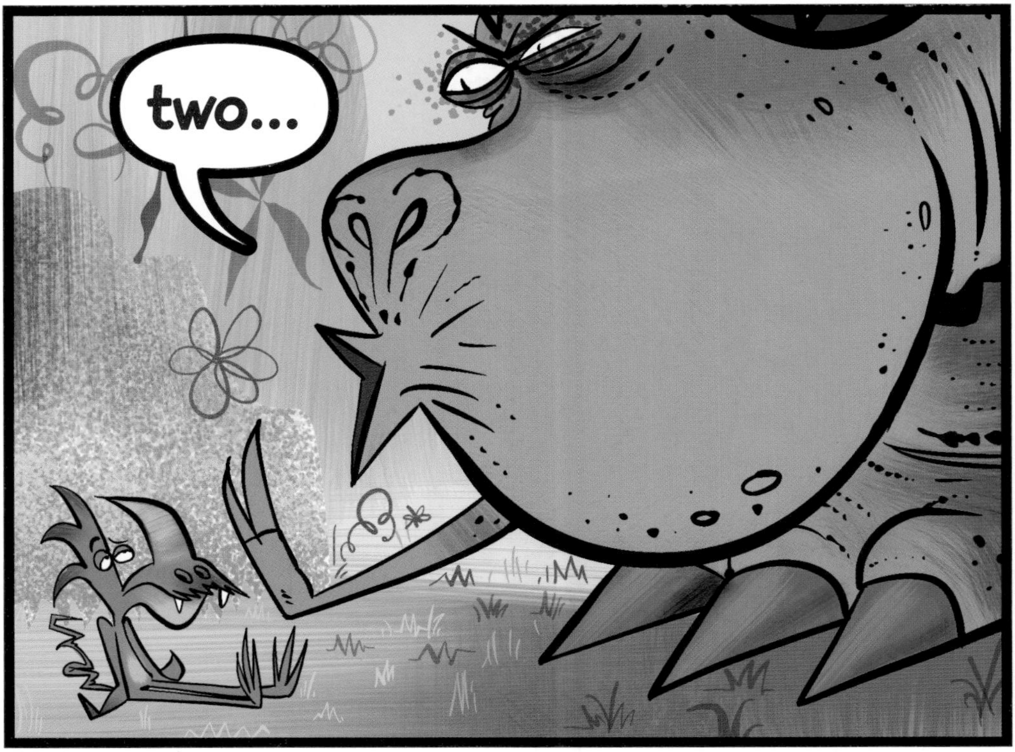
two...

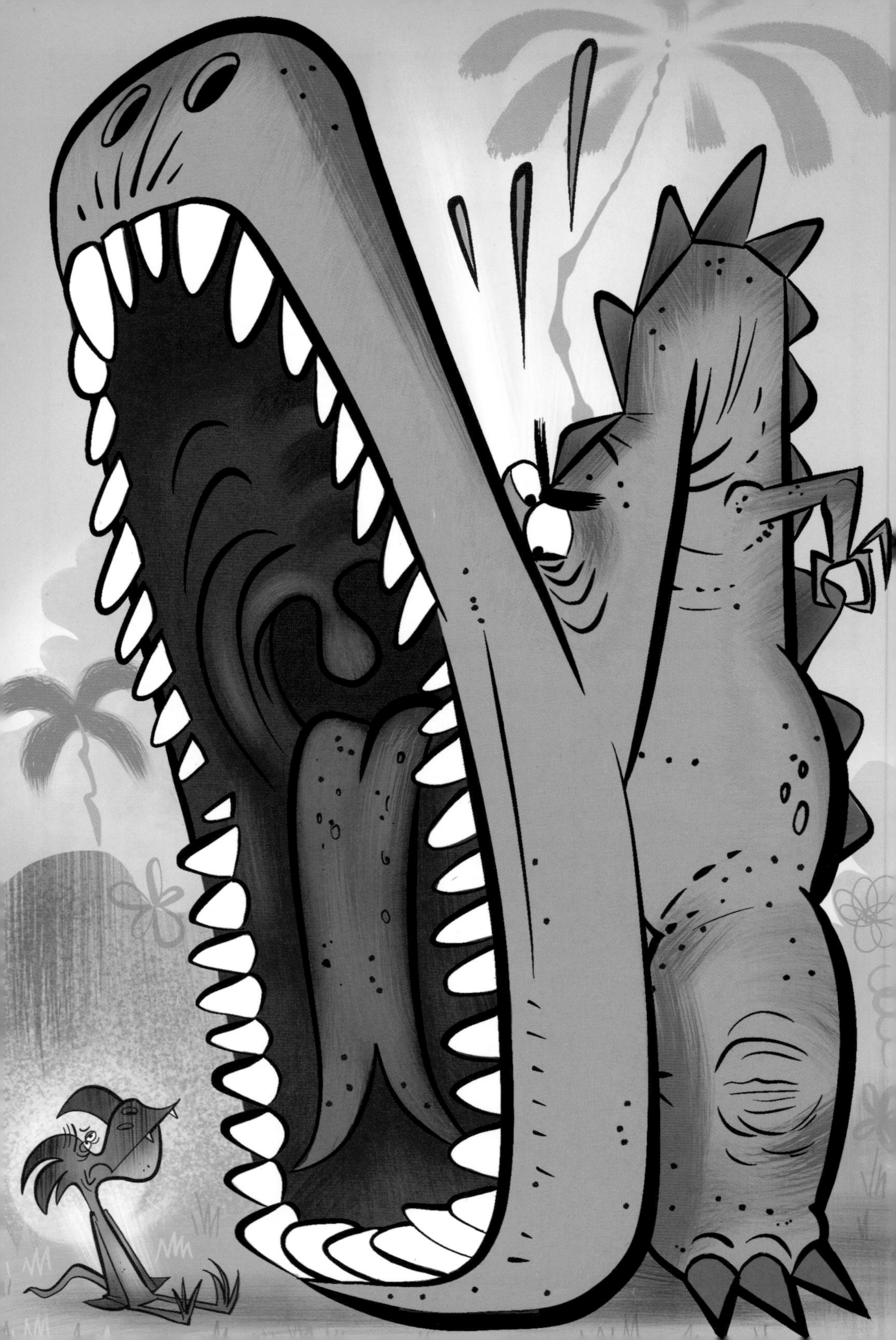

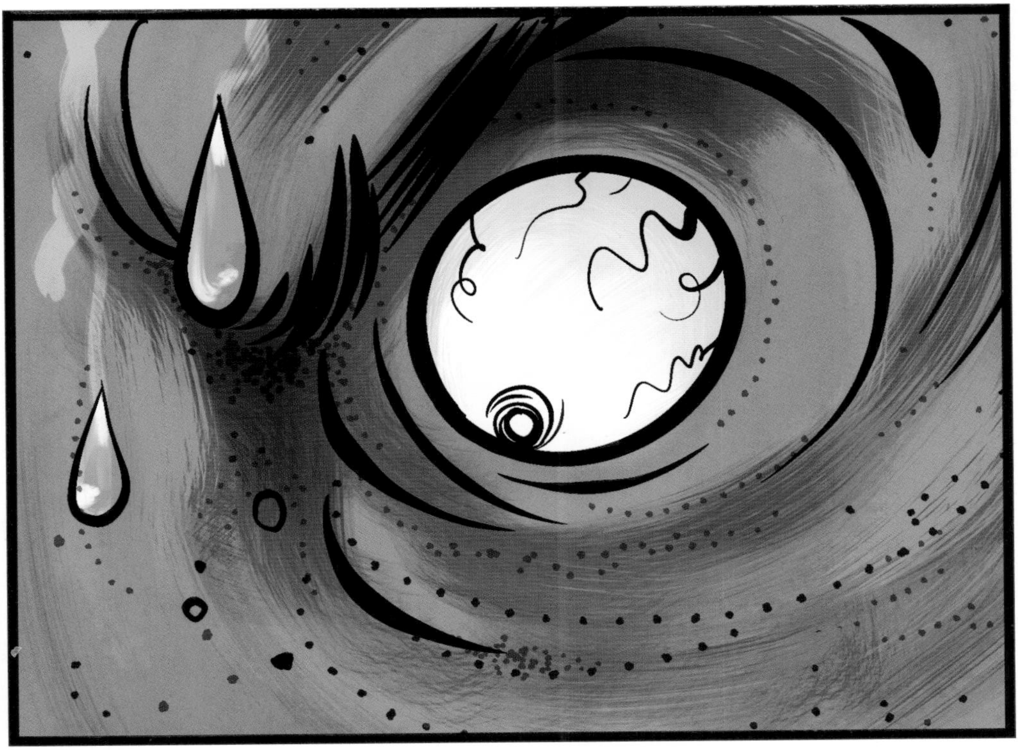

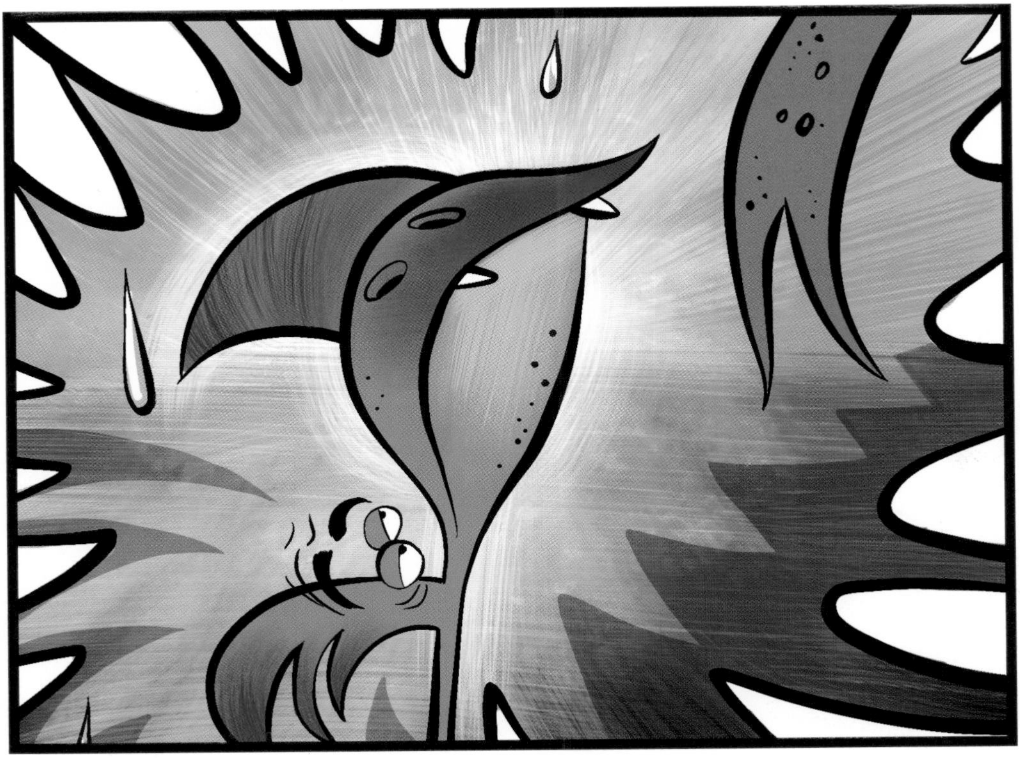

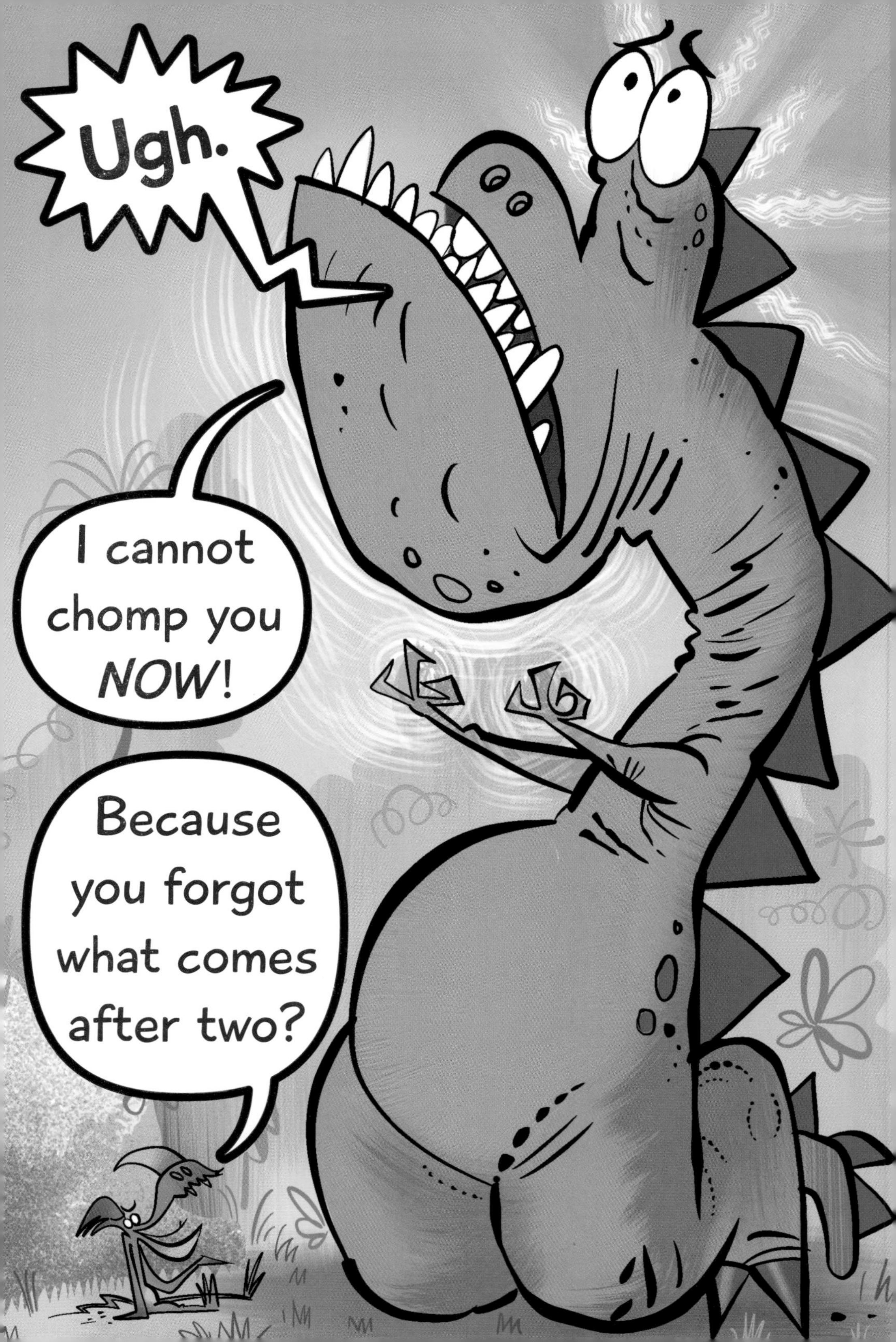
Ugh.
I cannot chomp you *NOW*!
Because you forgot what comes after two?

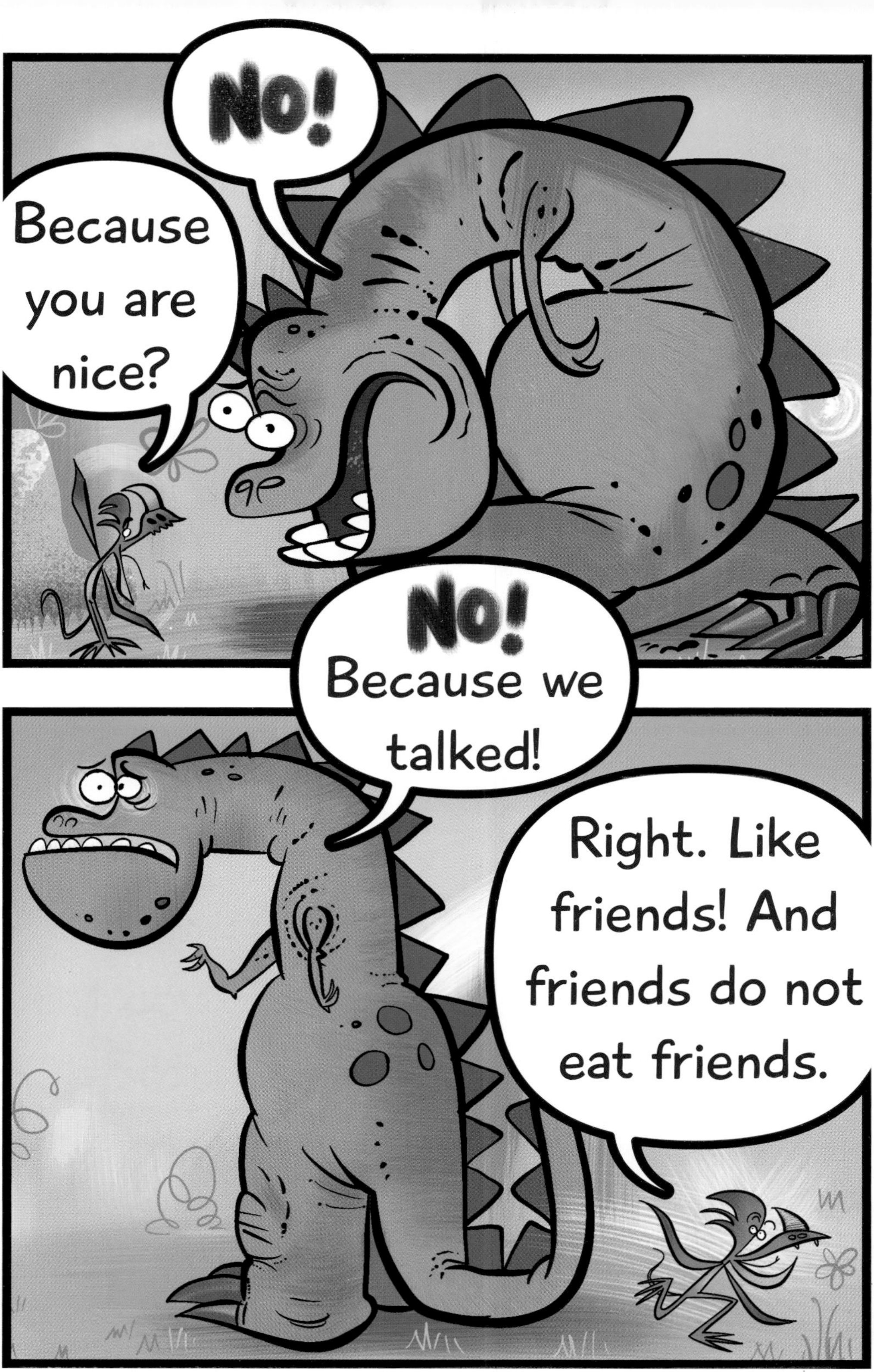
NO!
Because you are nice?
NO! Because we talked!
Right. Like friends! And friends do not eat friends.

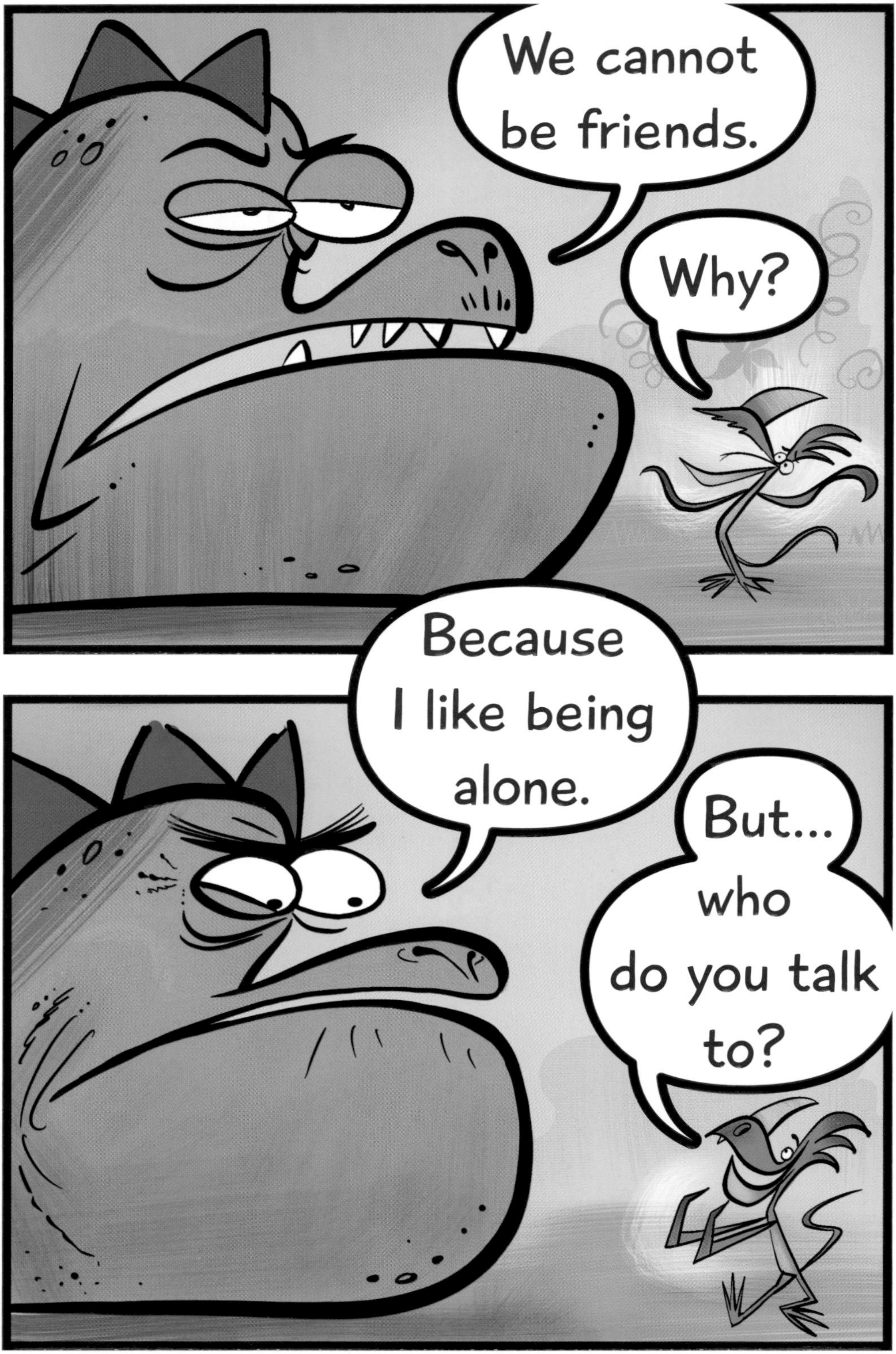
We cannot be friends.
Why?
Because I like being alone.
But... who do you talk to?

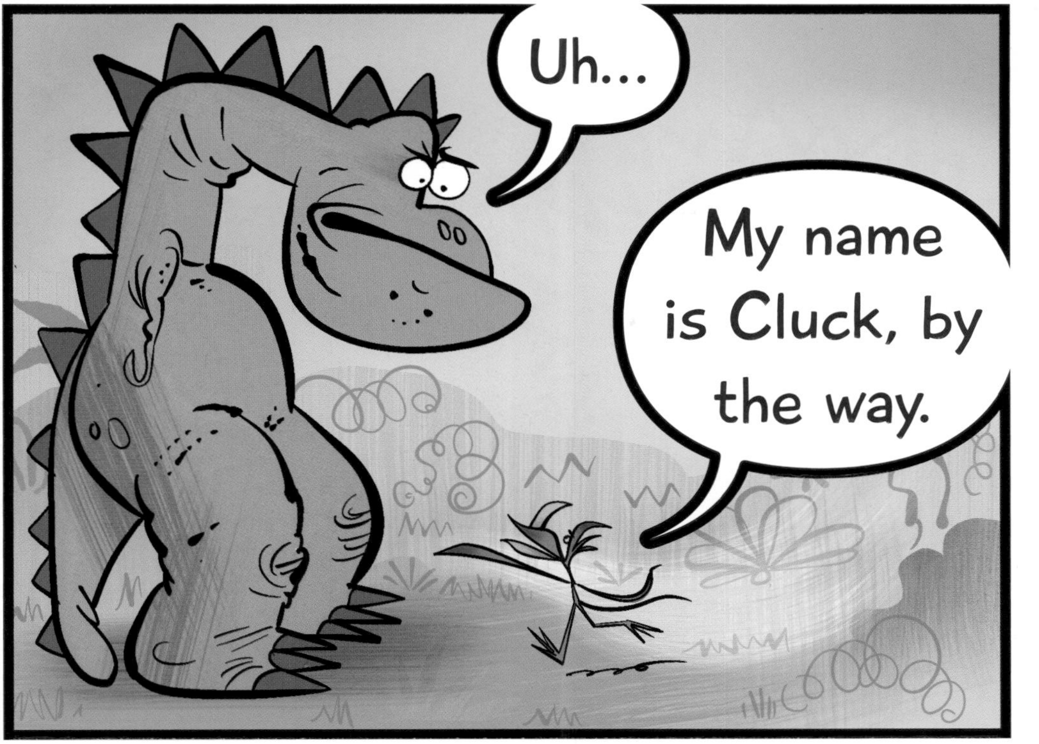
Uh...
My name is Cluck, by the way.
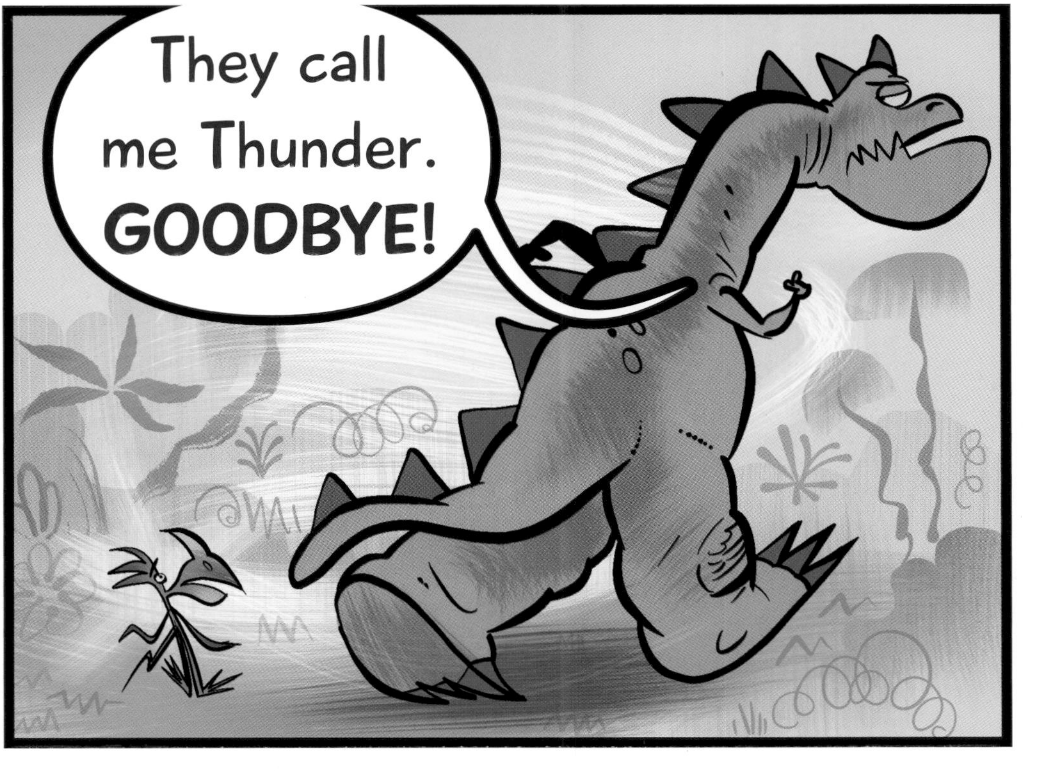
They call me Thunder. **GOODBYE!**

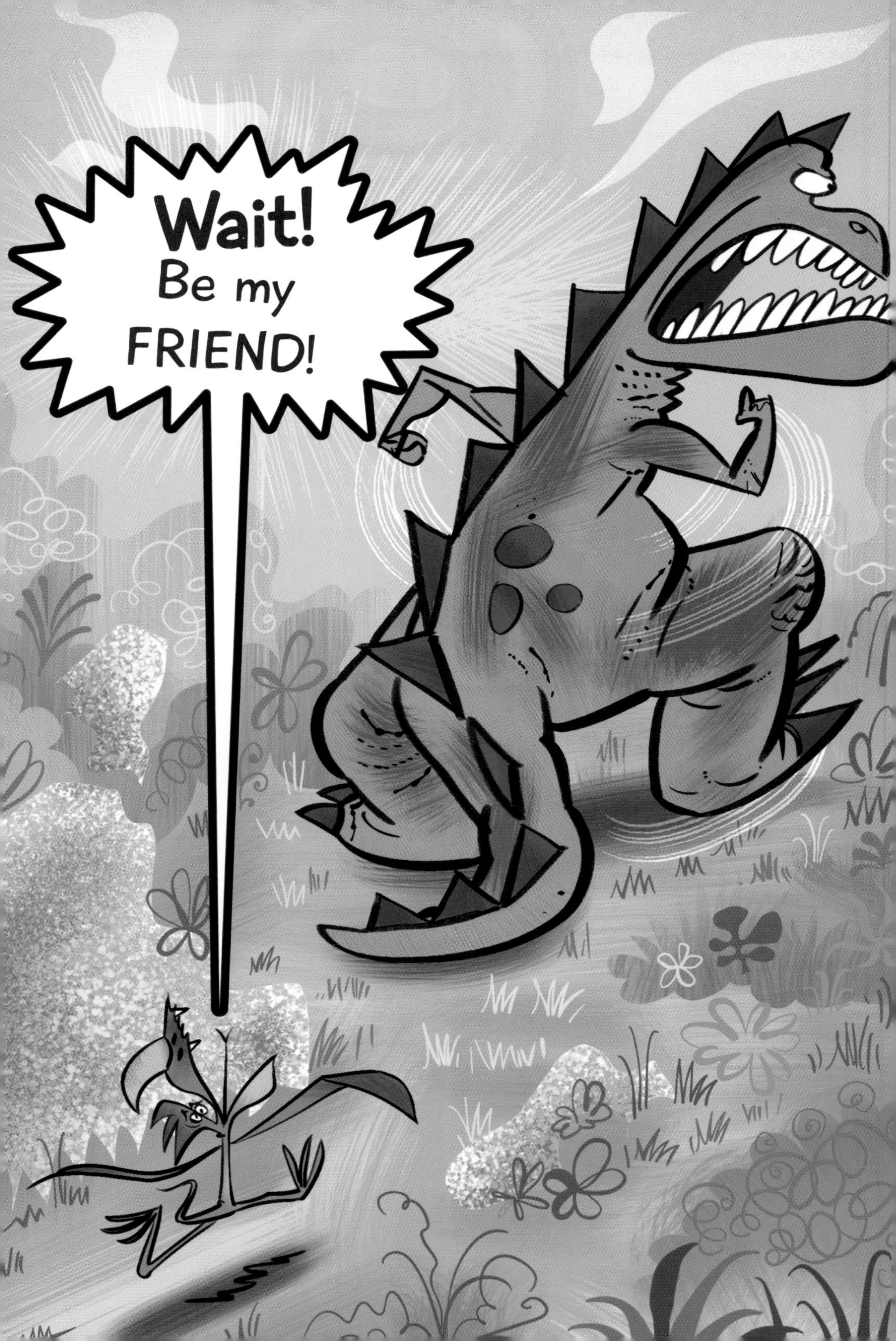
Wait! Be my FRIEND!

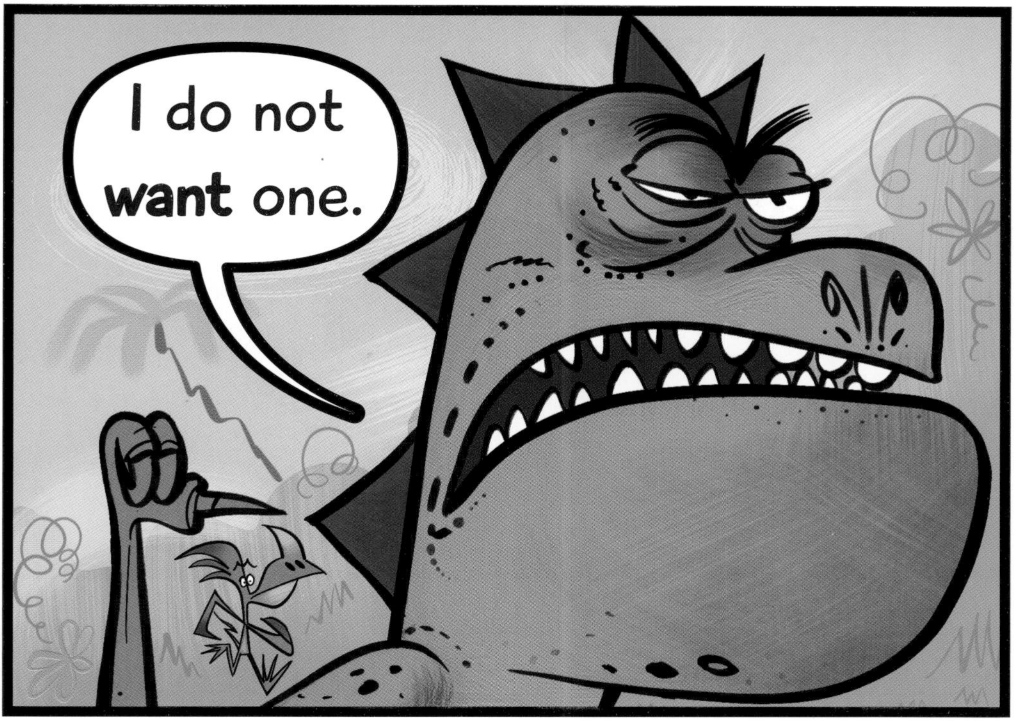
I do not **want** one.

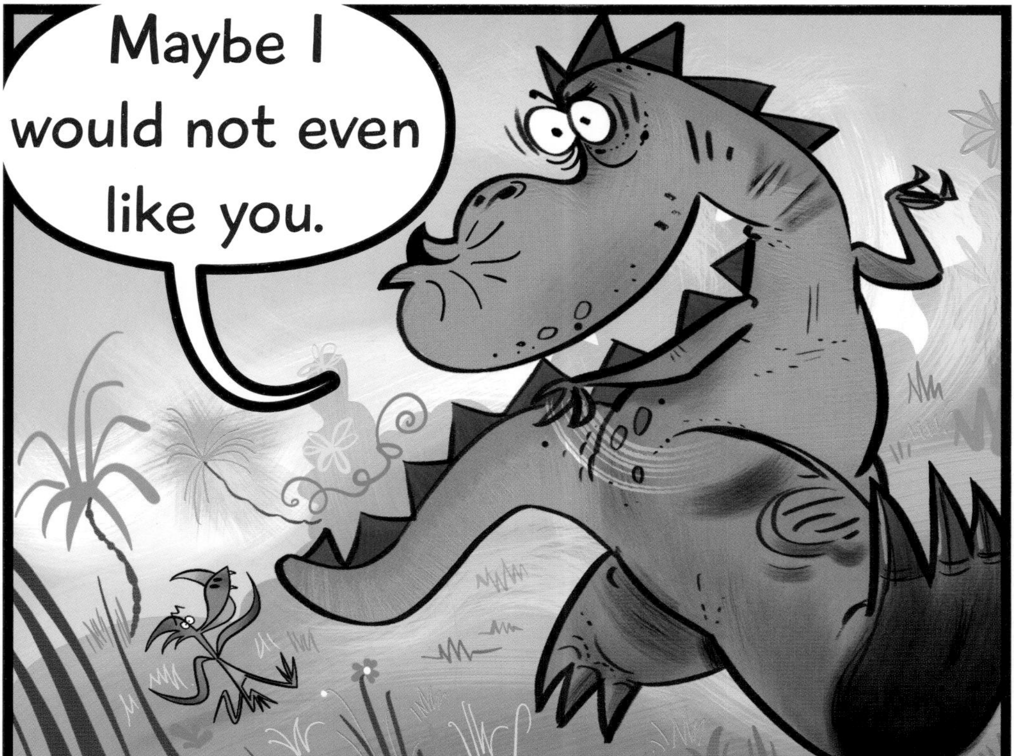
Maybe I would not even like you.

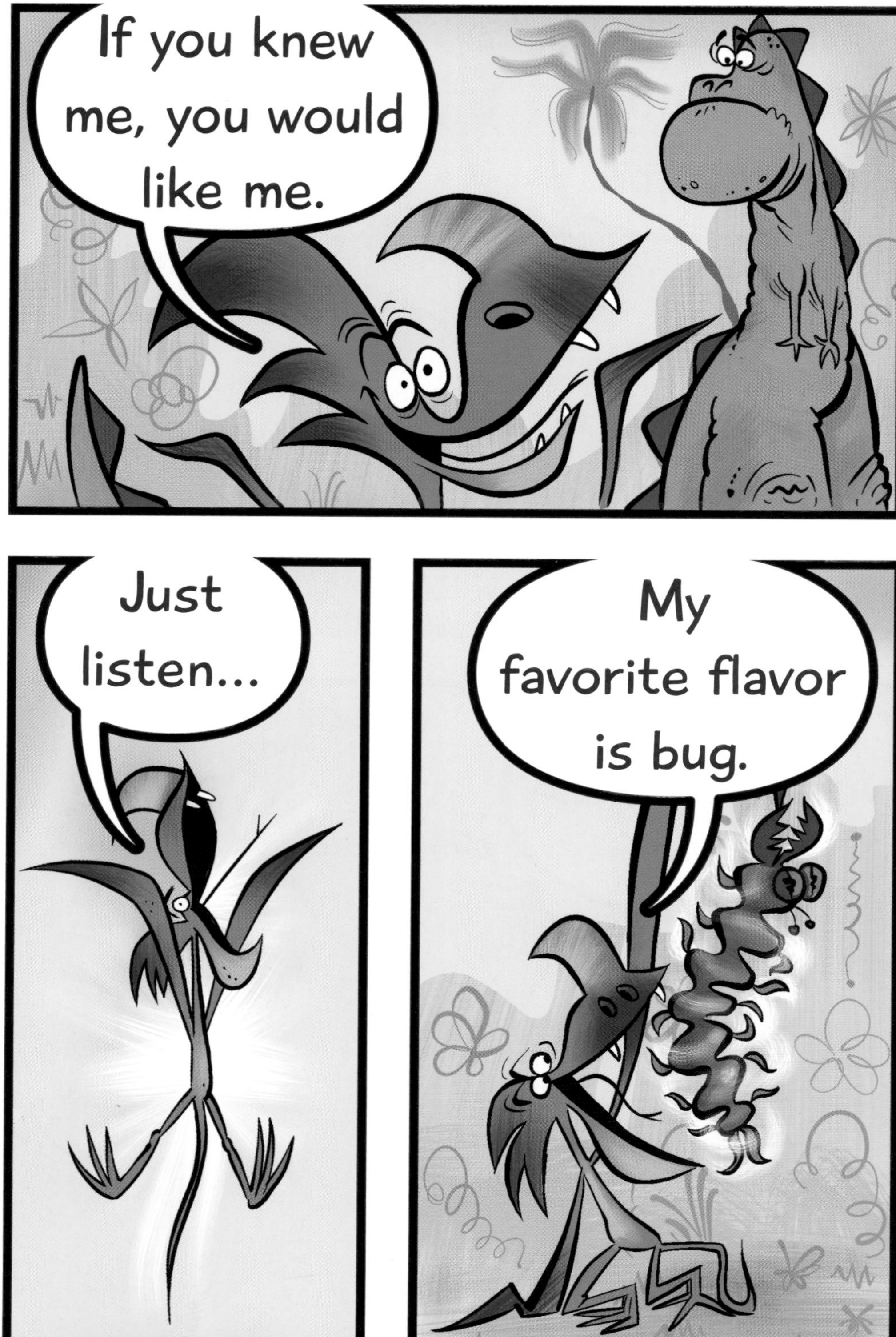
If you knew me, you would like me.
Just listen...
My favorite flavor is bug.

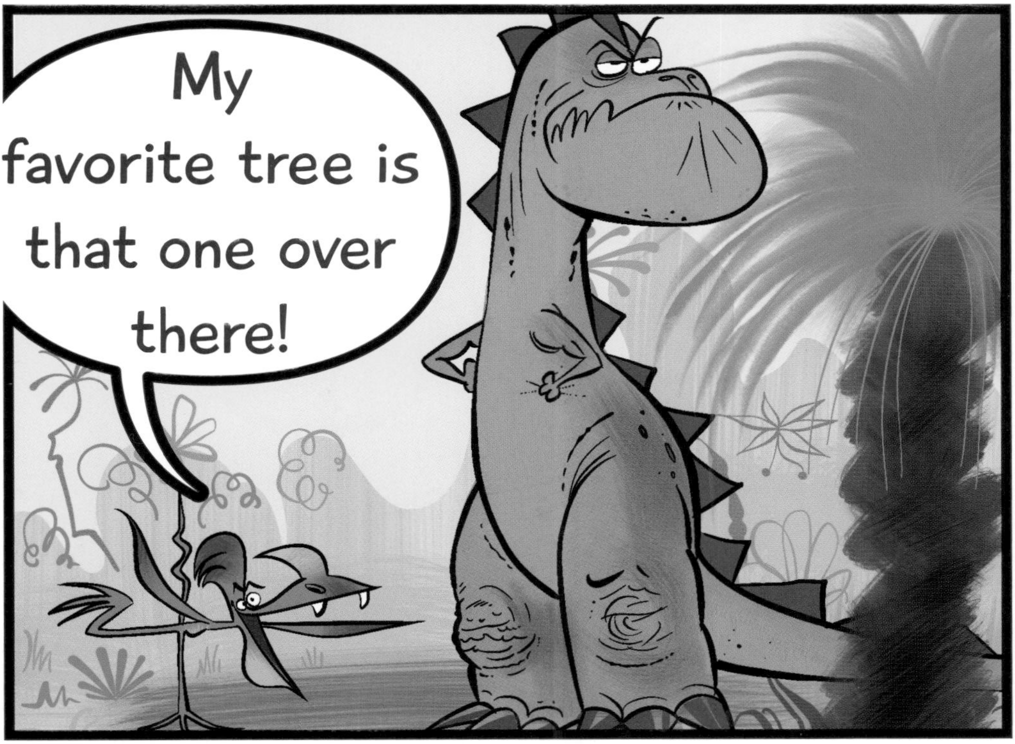
My favorite tree is that one over there!

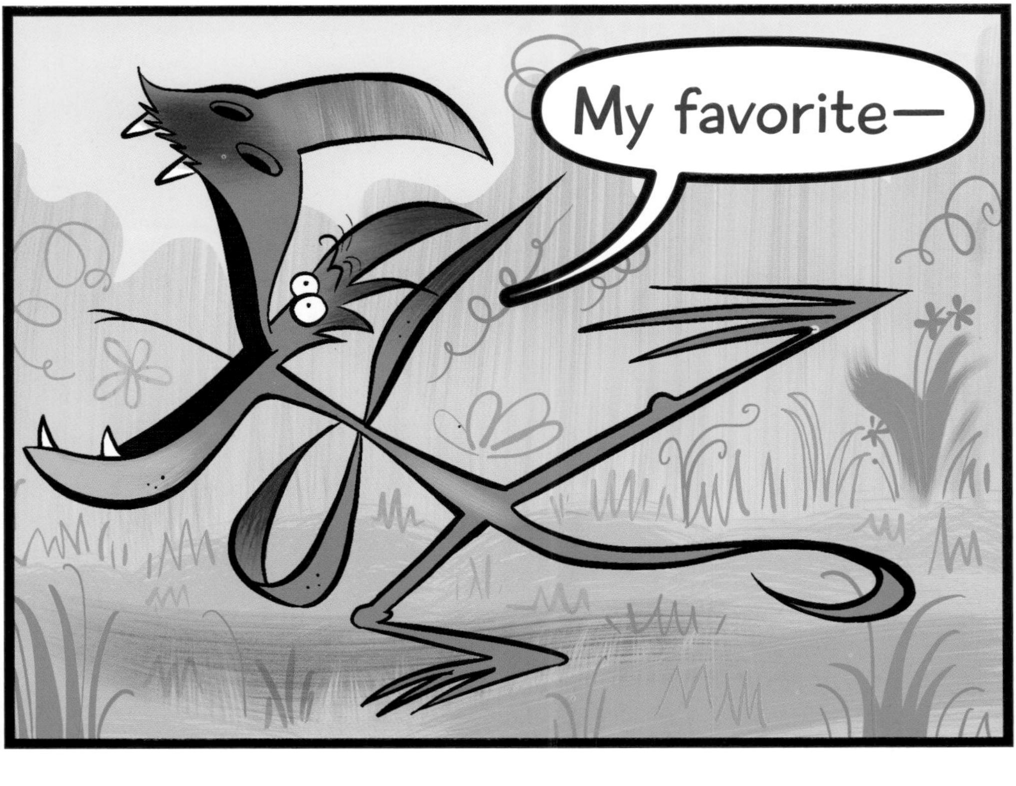
My favorite—

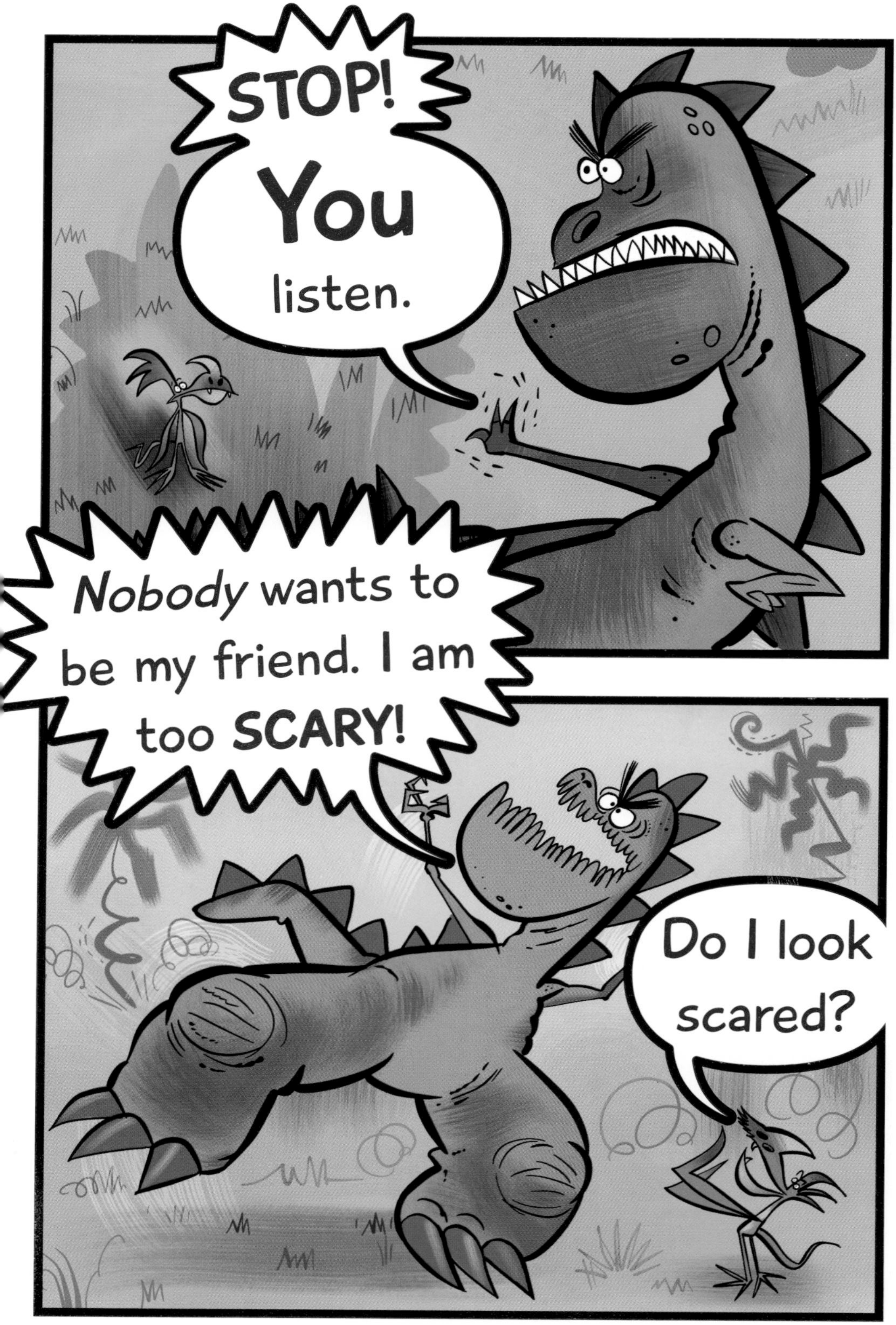
STOP!
You
You listen.
Nobody wants to be my friend. I am too SCARY!
Do I look scared?

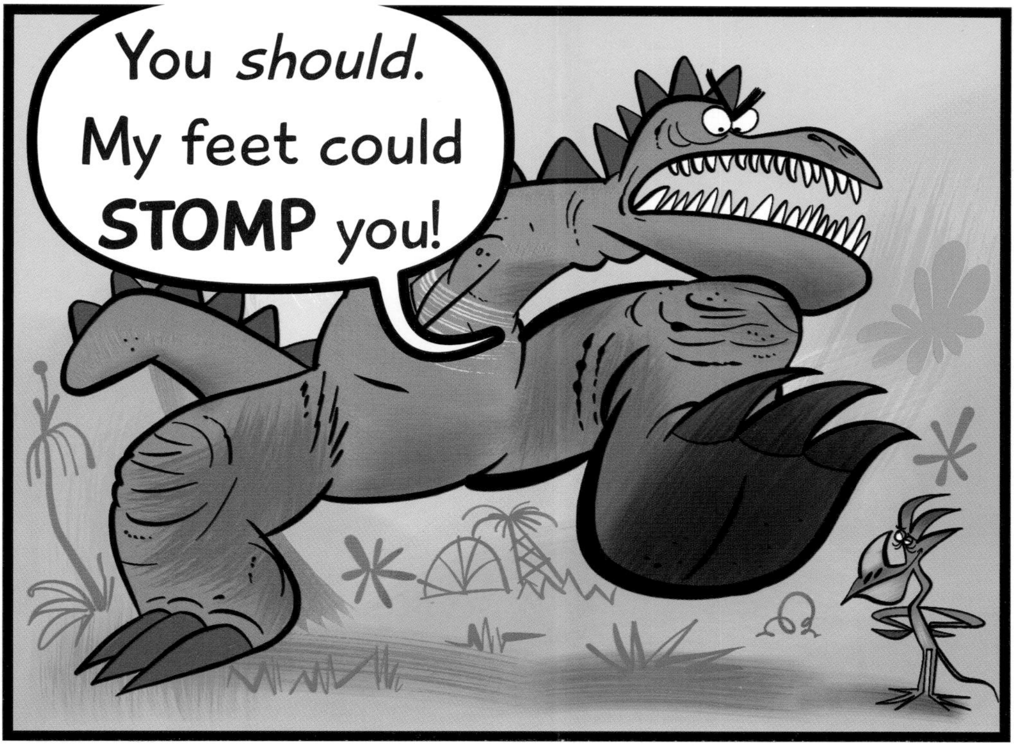
You *should.* My feet could **STOMP** you!

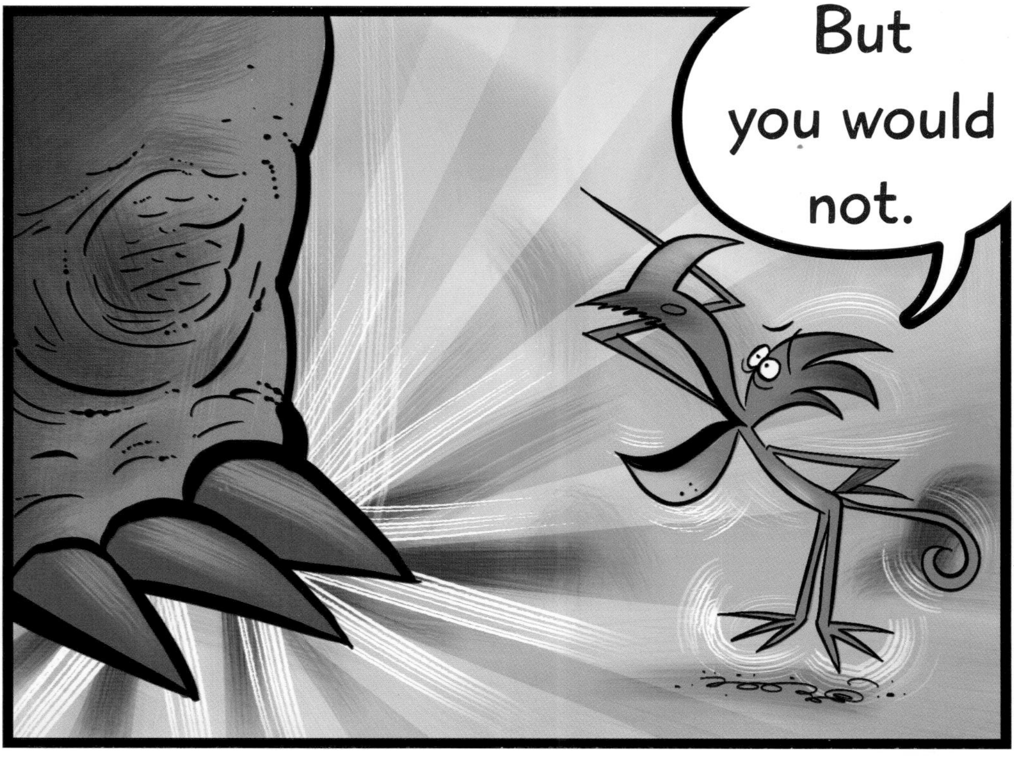
But you would not.

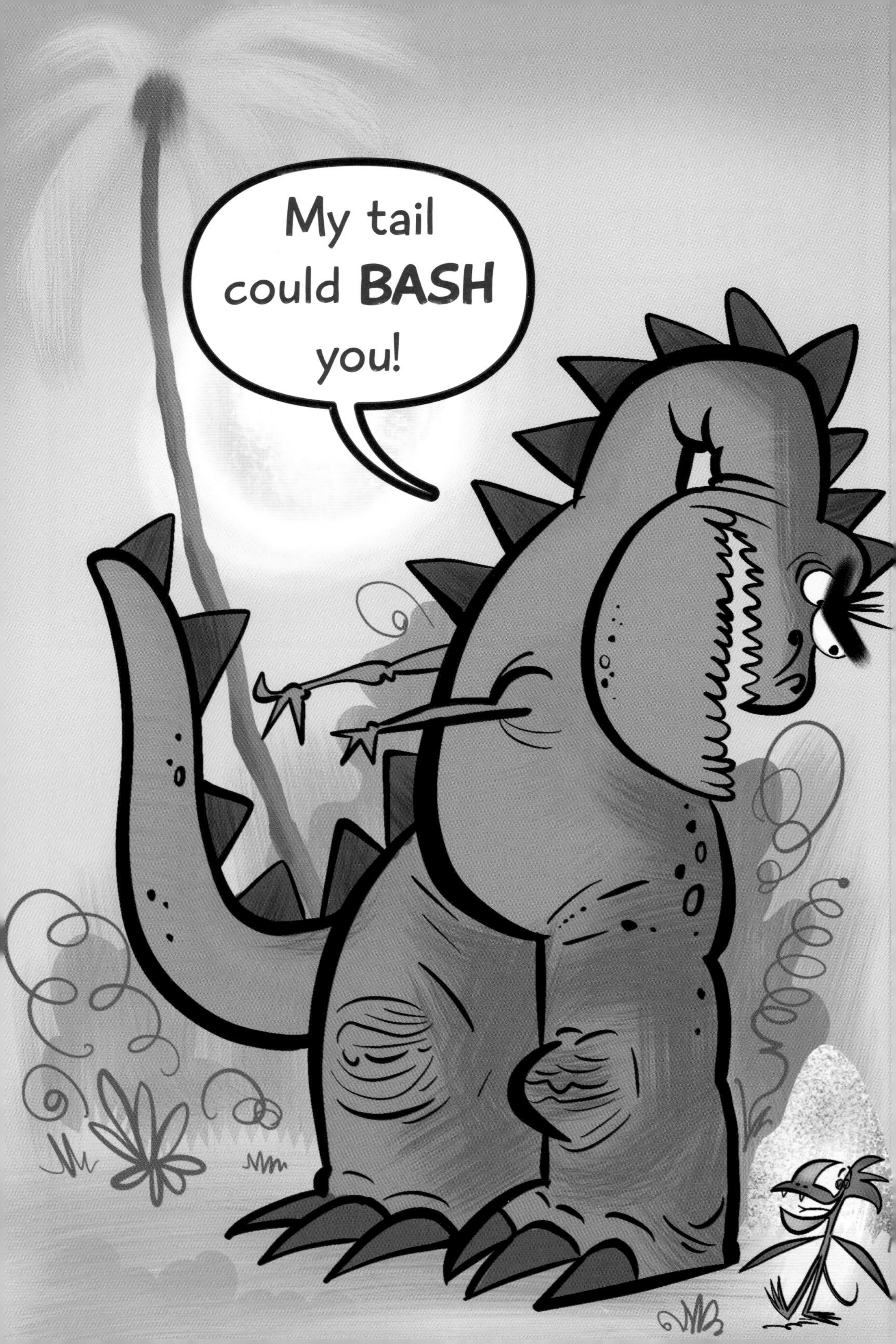
My tail could **BASH** you!

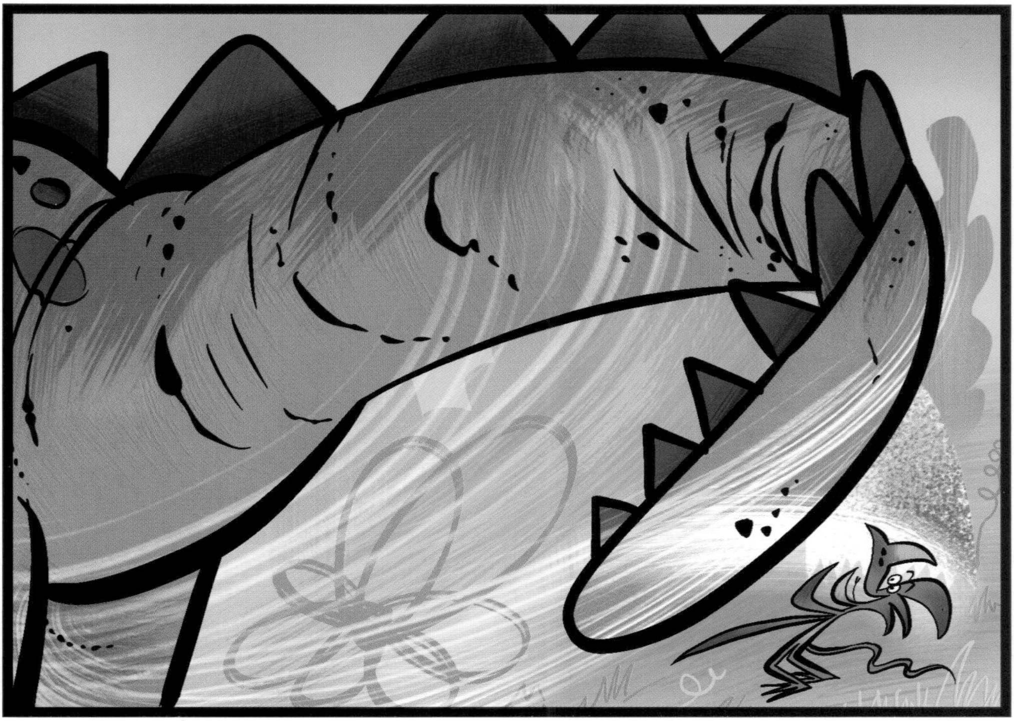

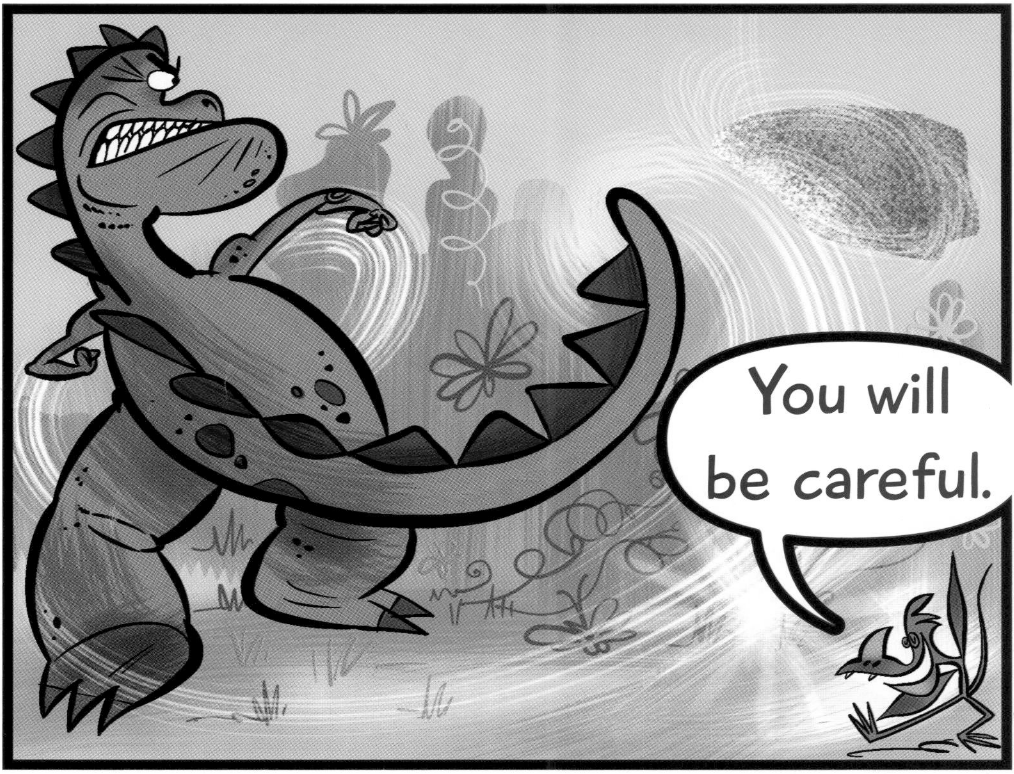
You will
be careful.

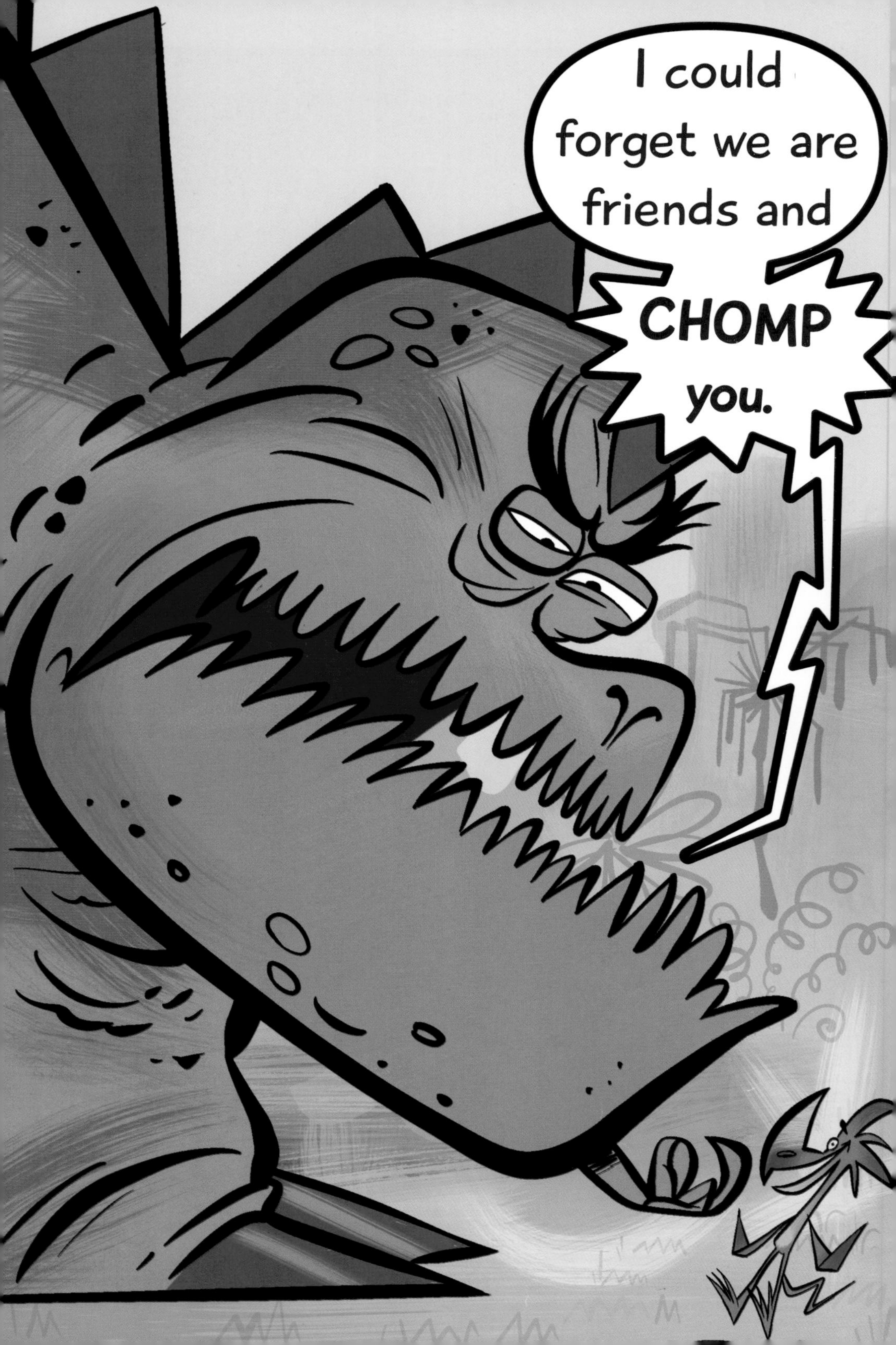
I could forget we are friends and
CHOMP you.

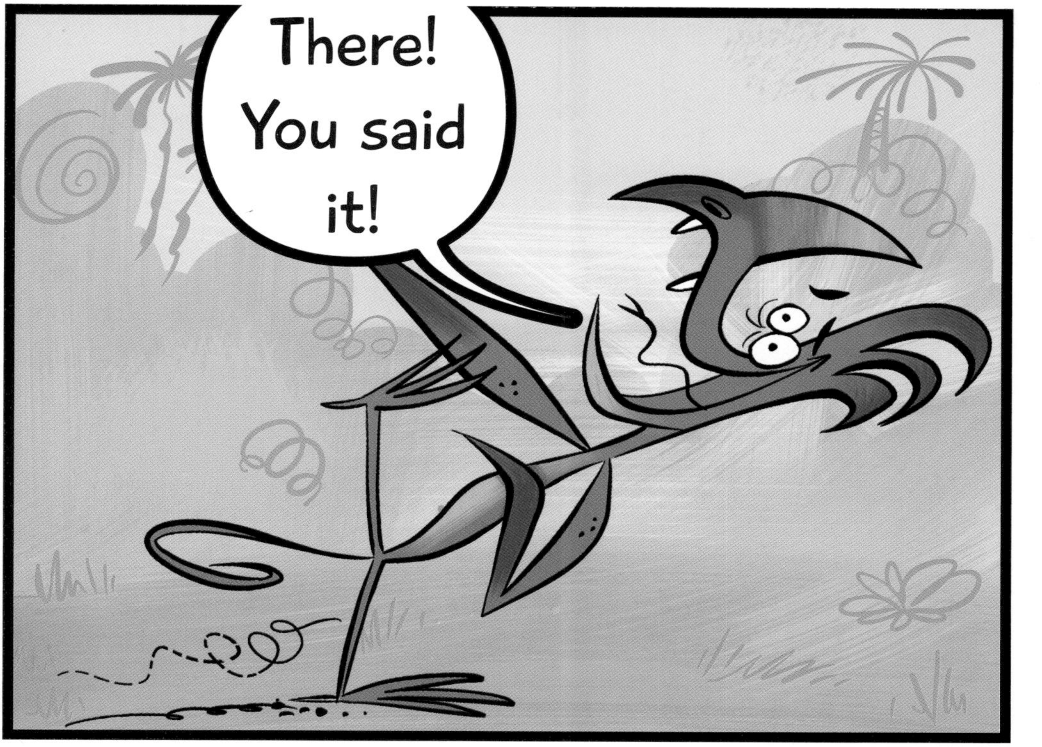
There! You said it!

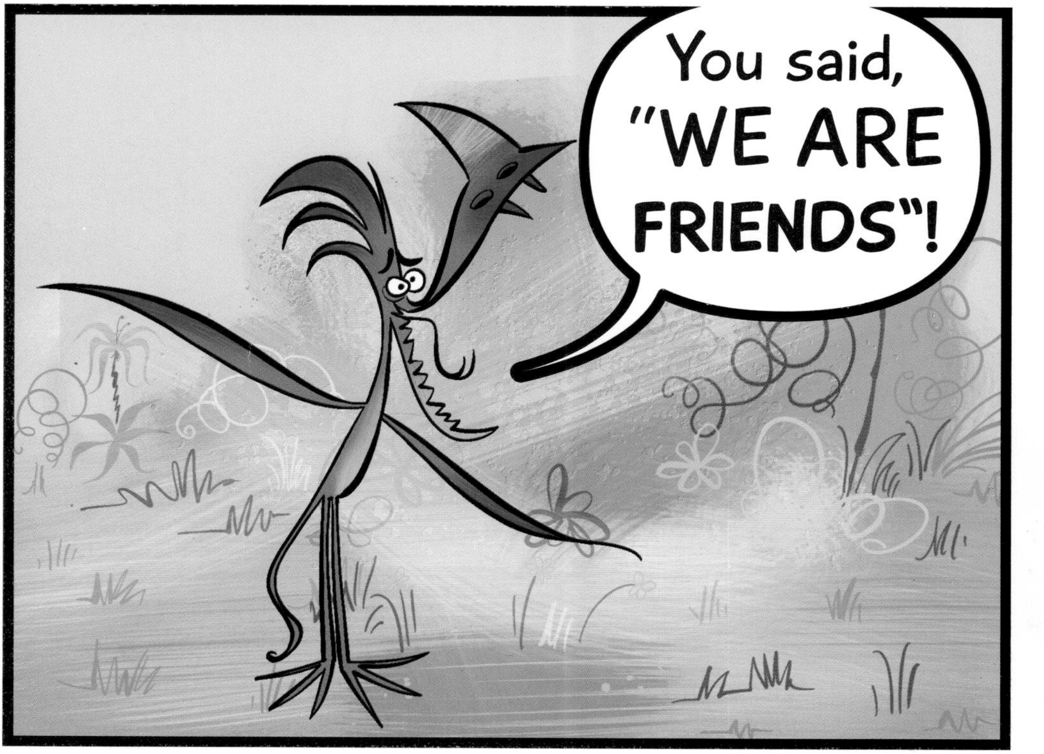
You said, "WE ARE FRIENDS"!

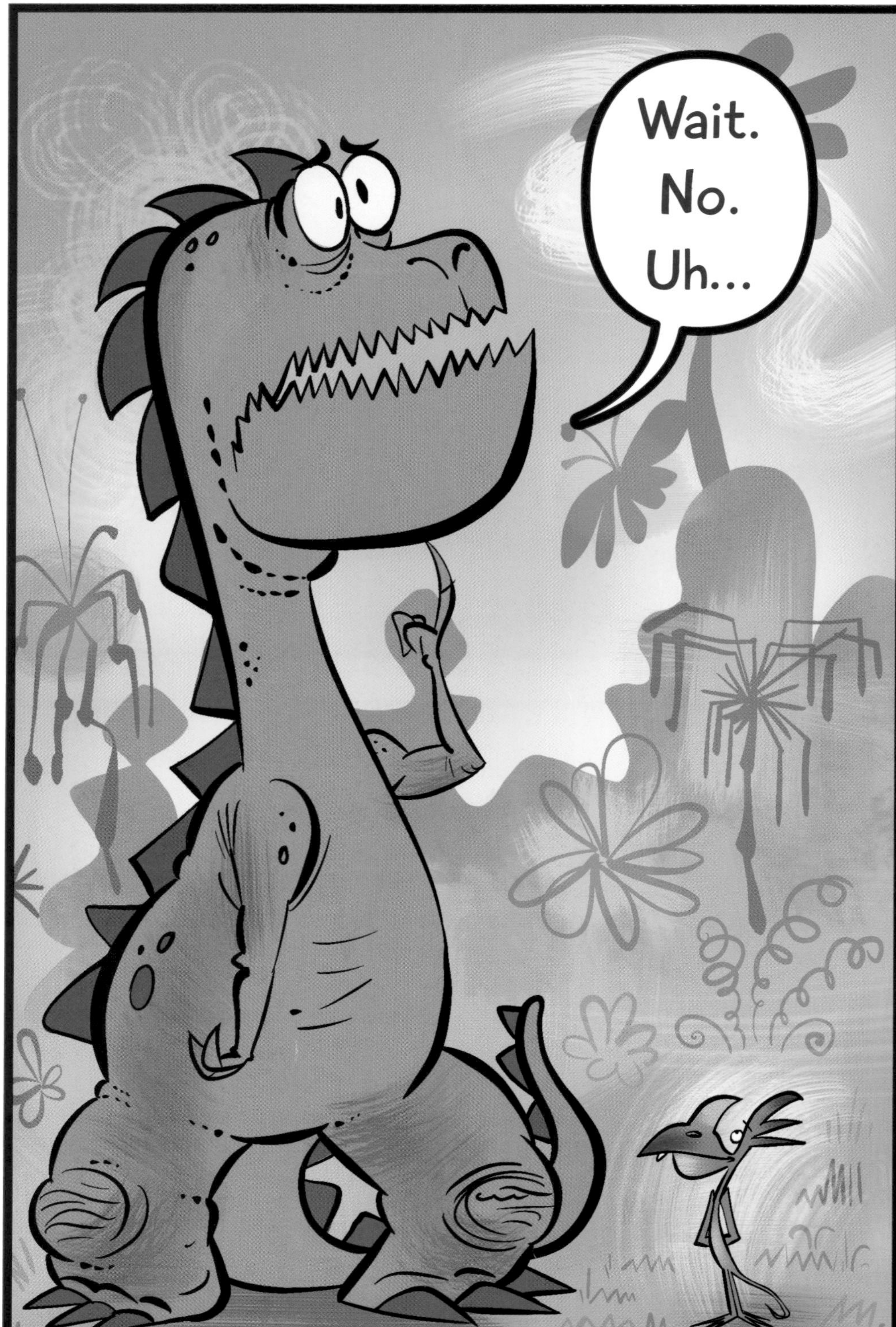
Wait.
No.
Uh...

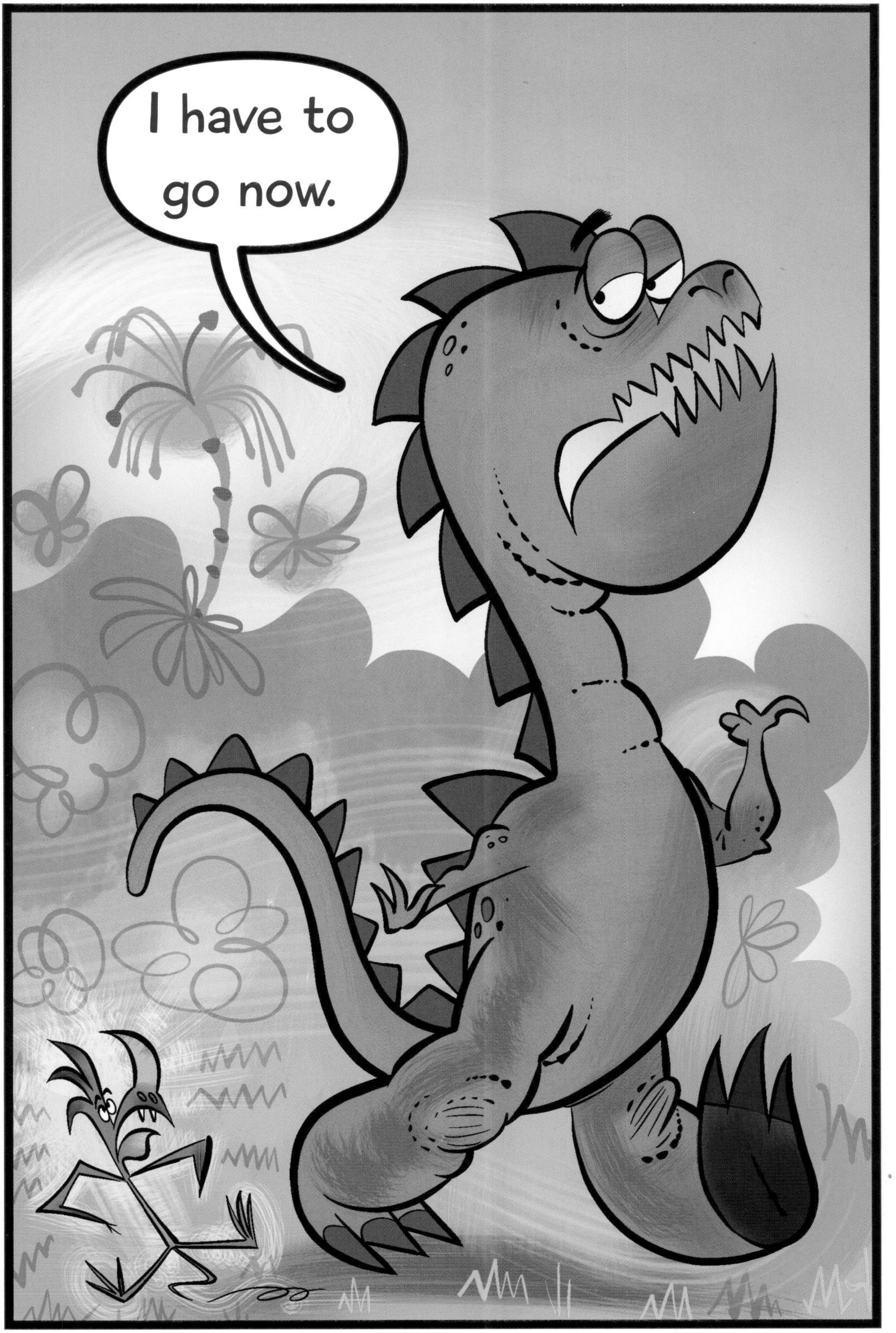
I have to go now.

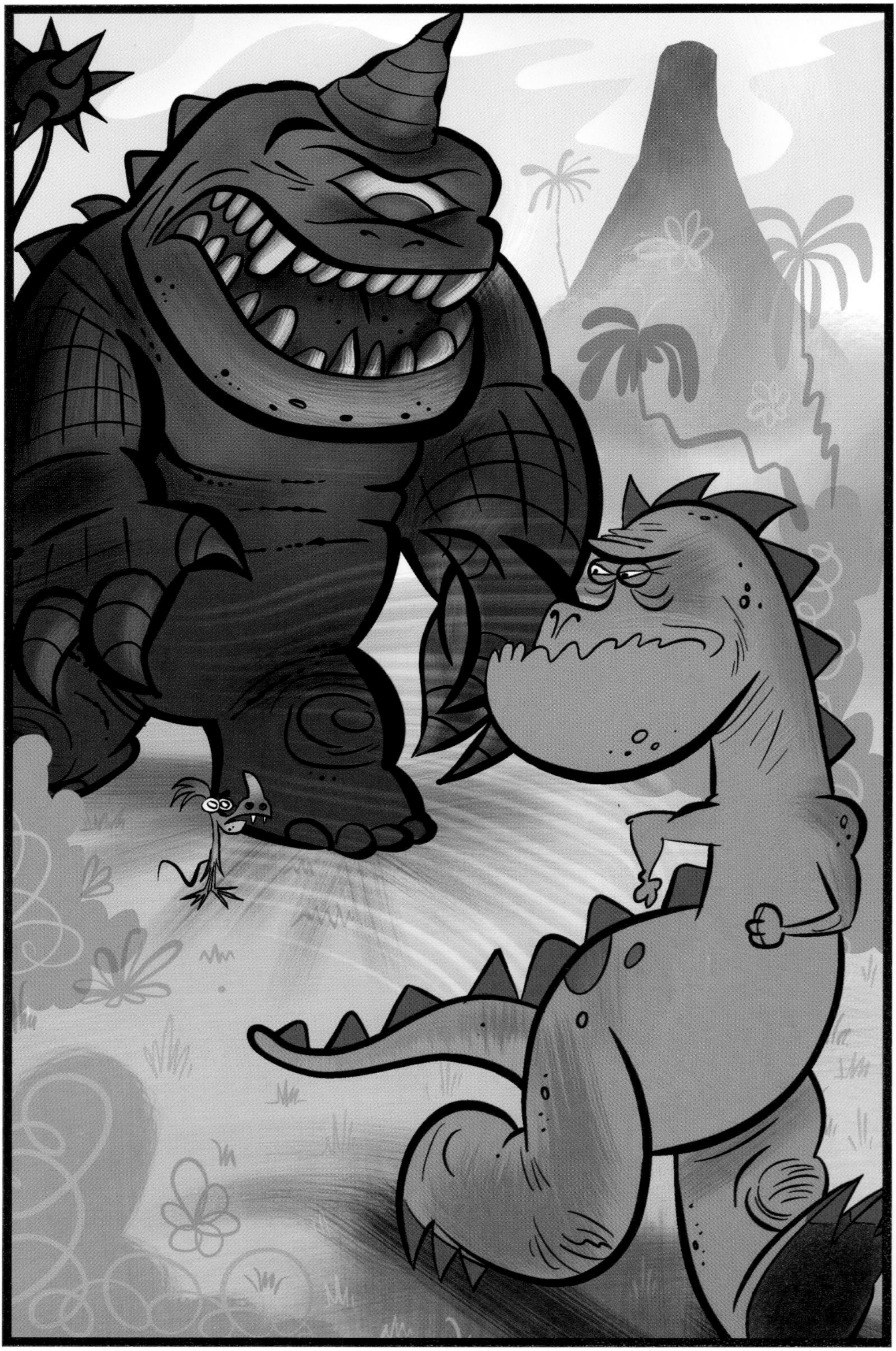

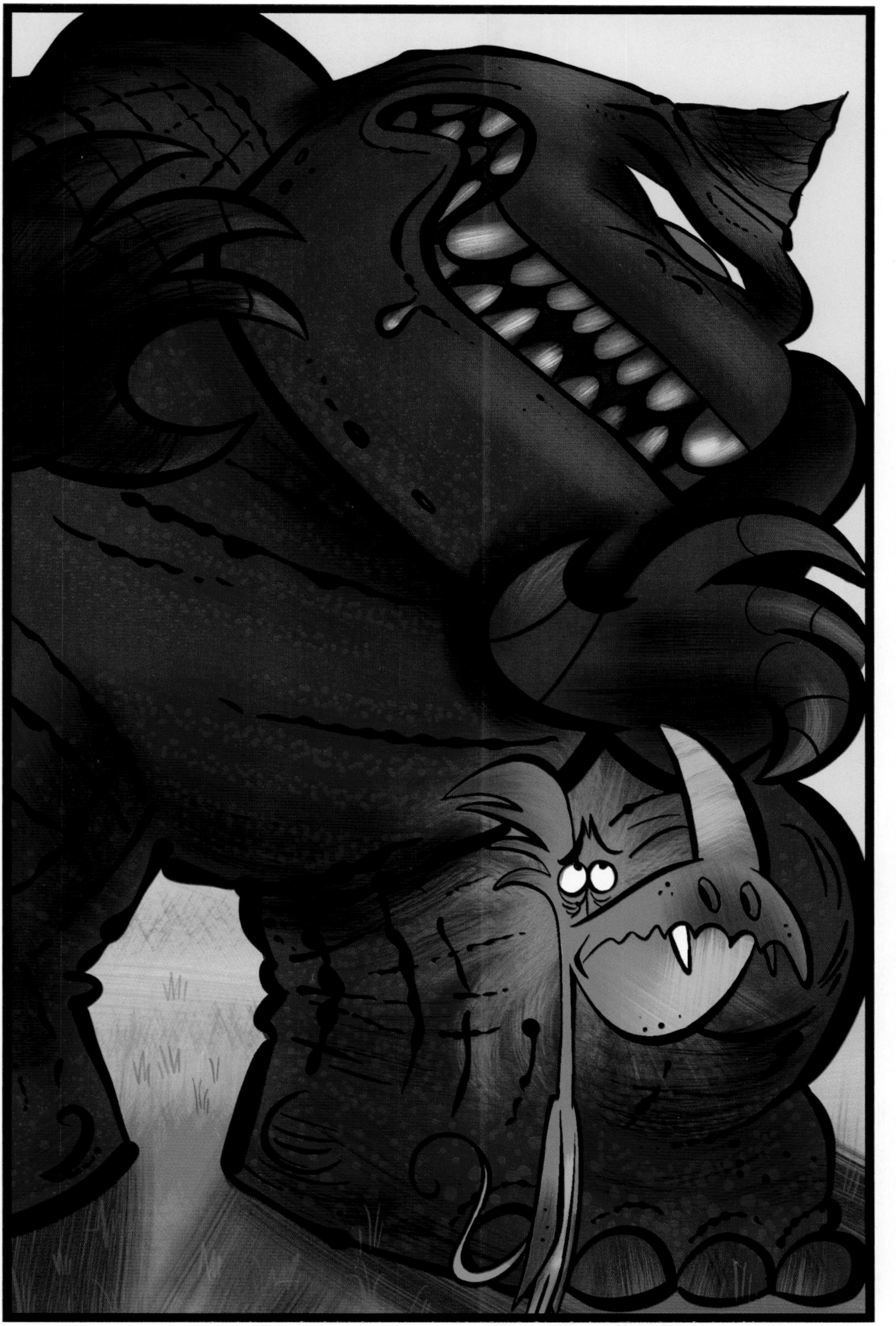

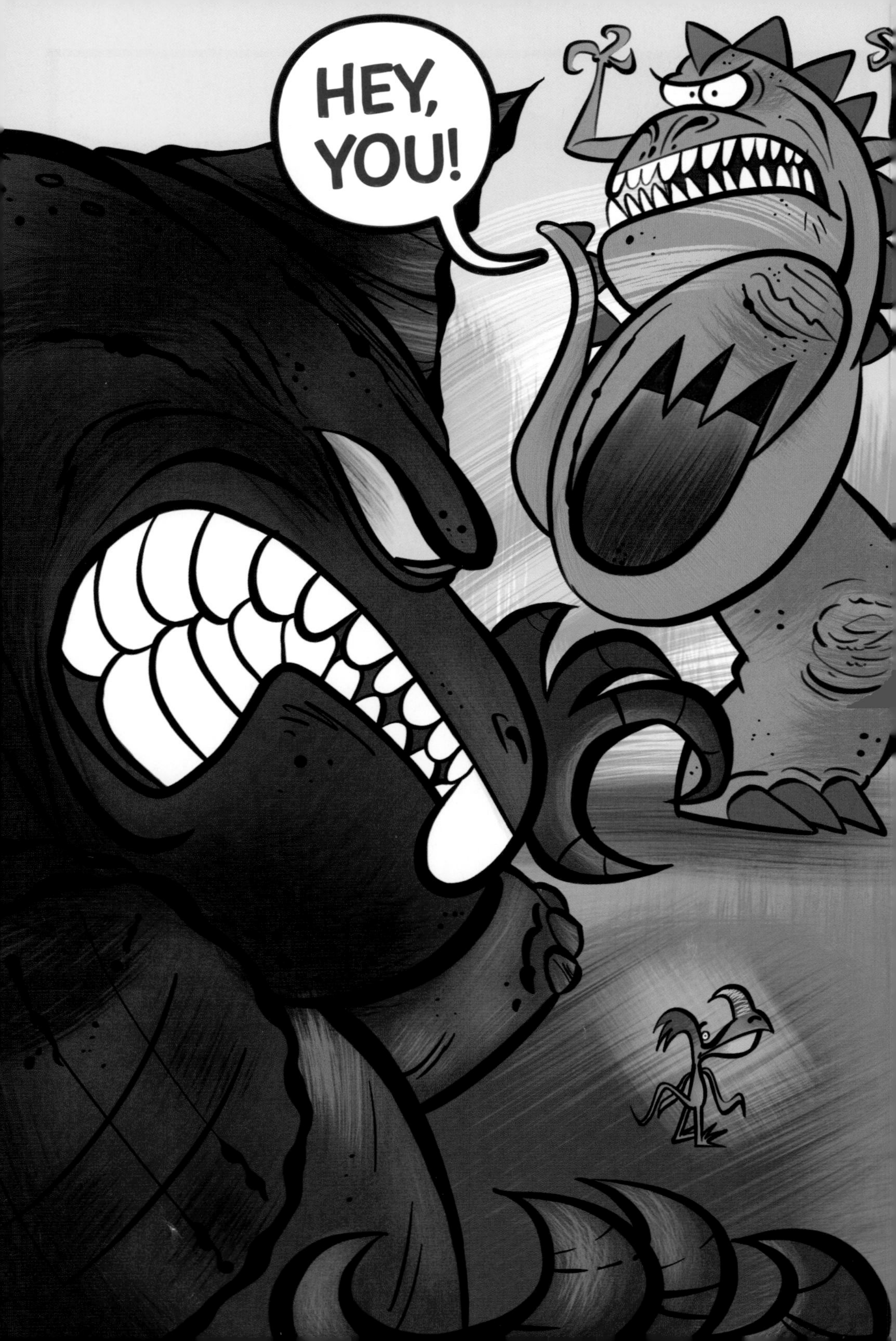
HEY, YOU!

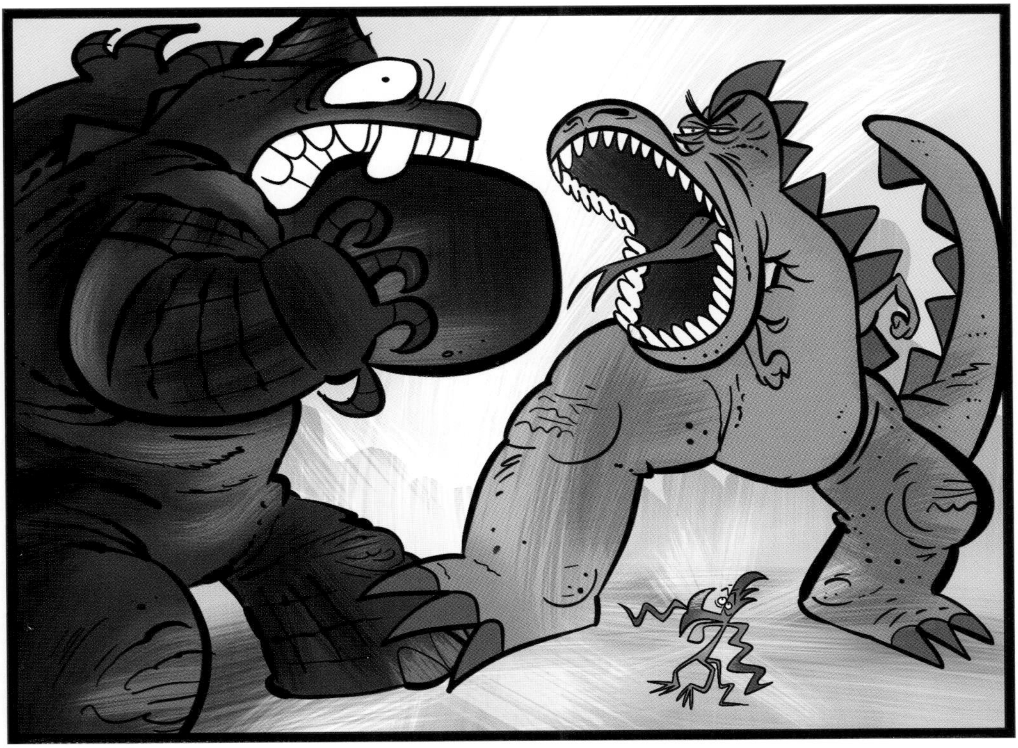
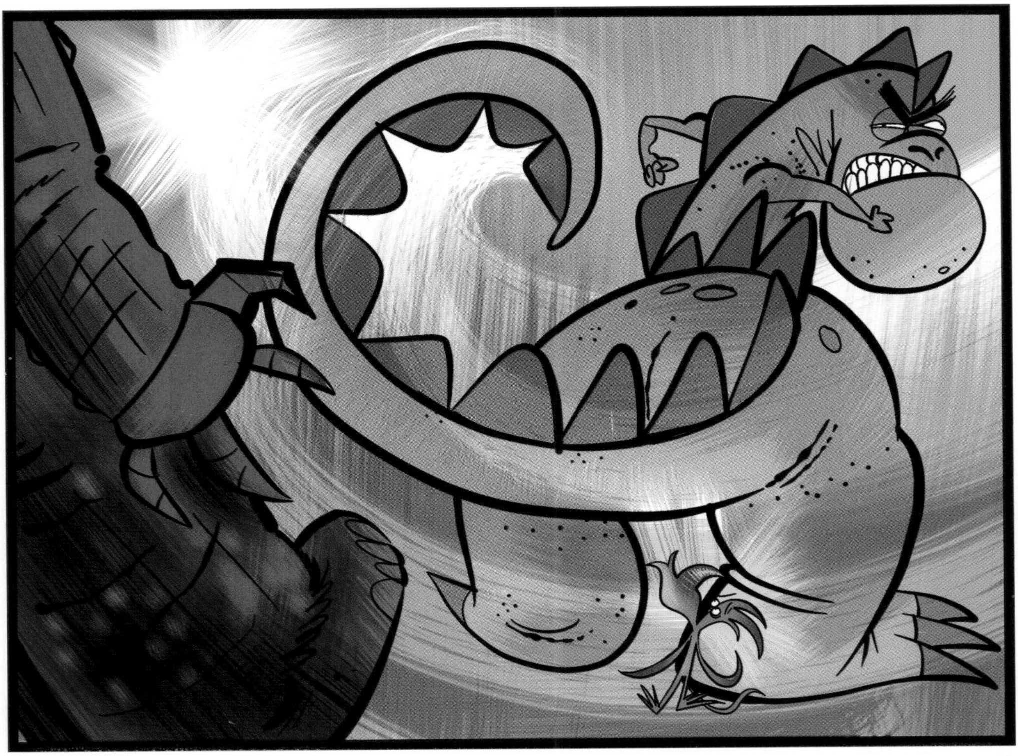

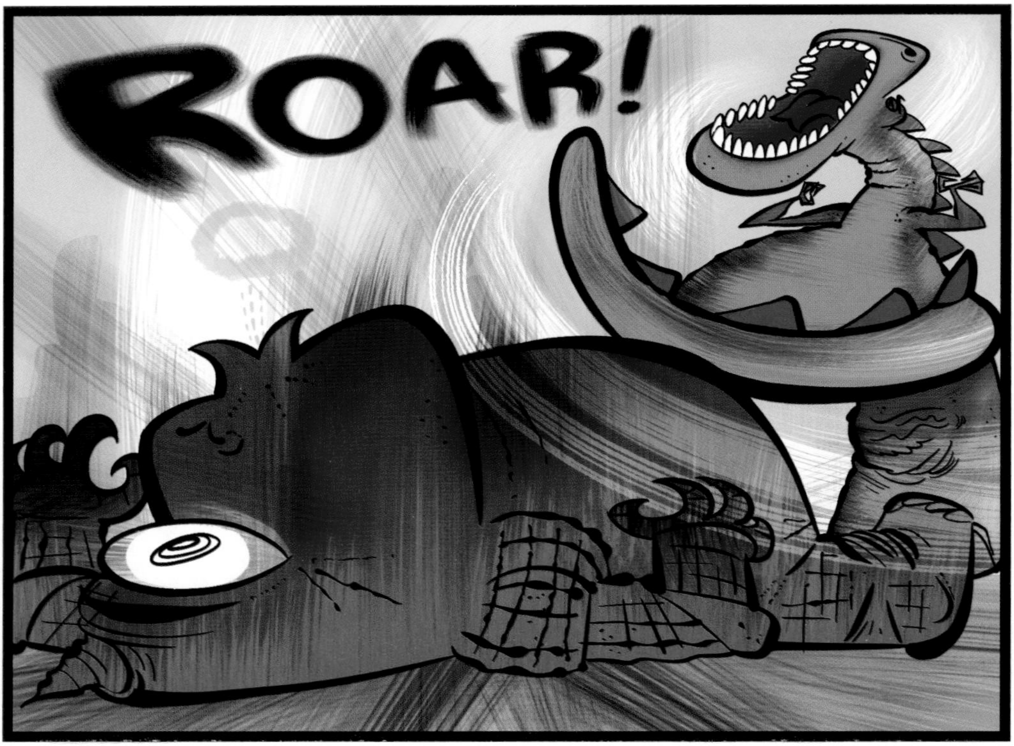
ROAR!

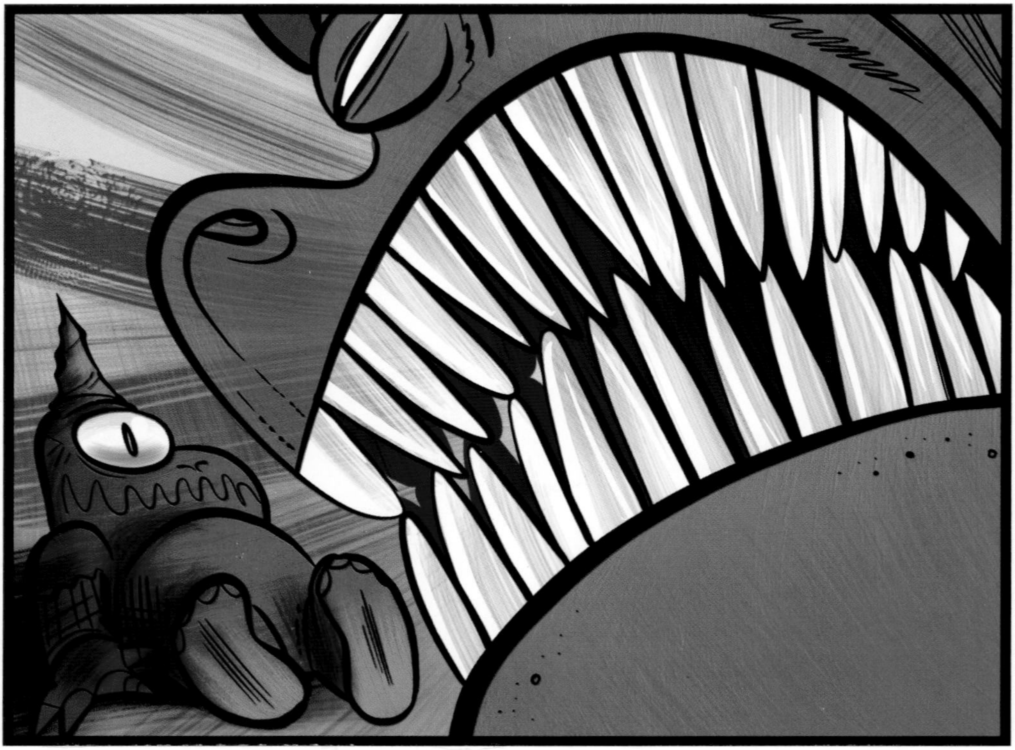

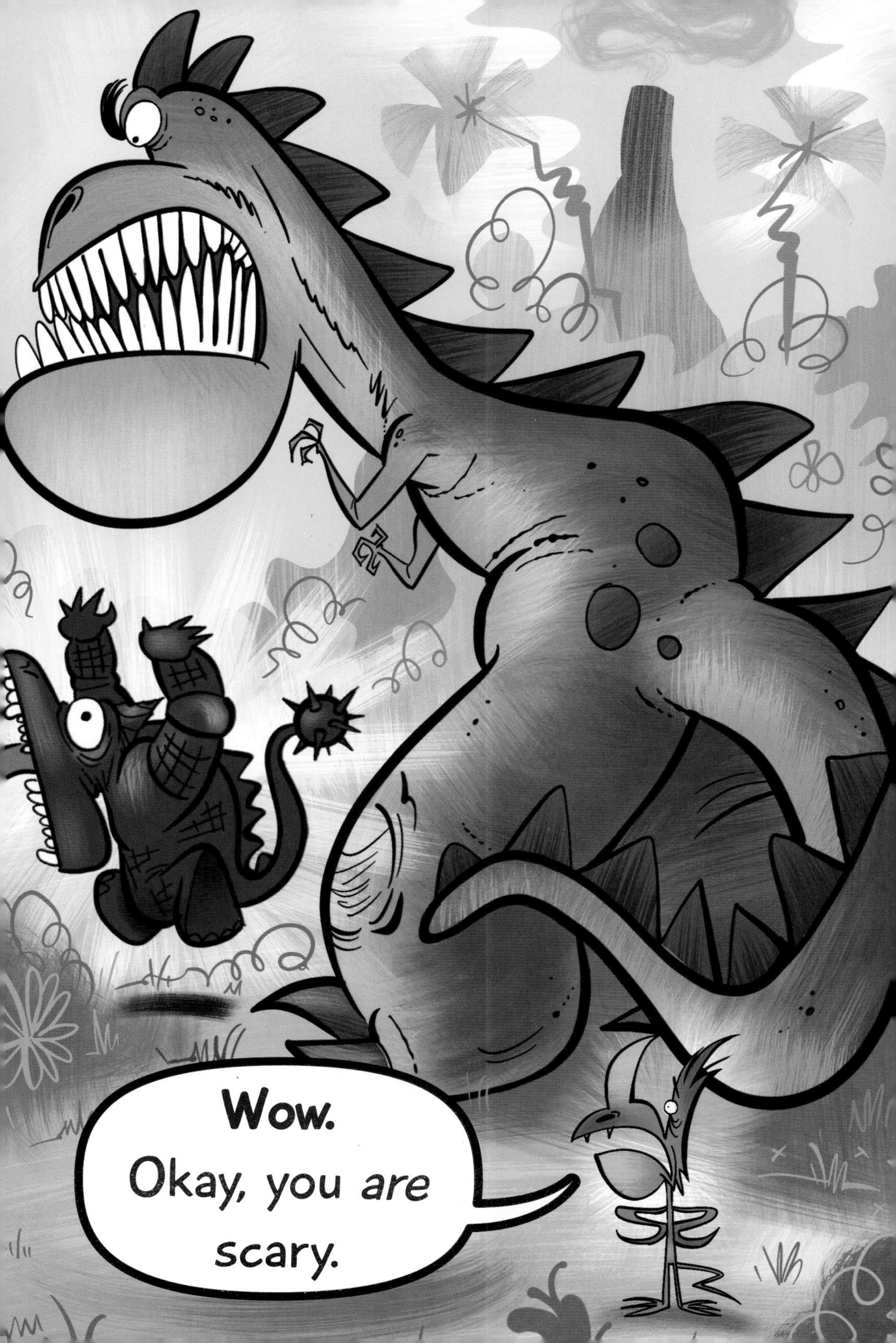
Wow.
Okay, you *are* scary.

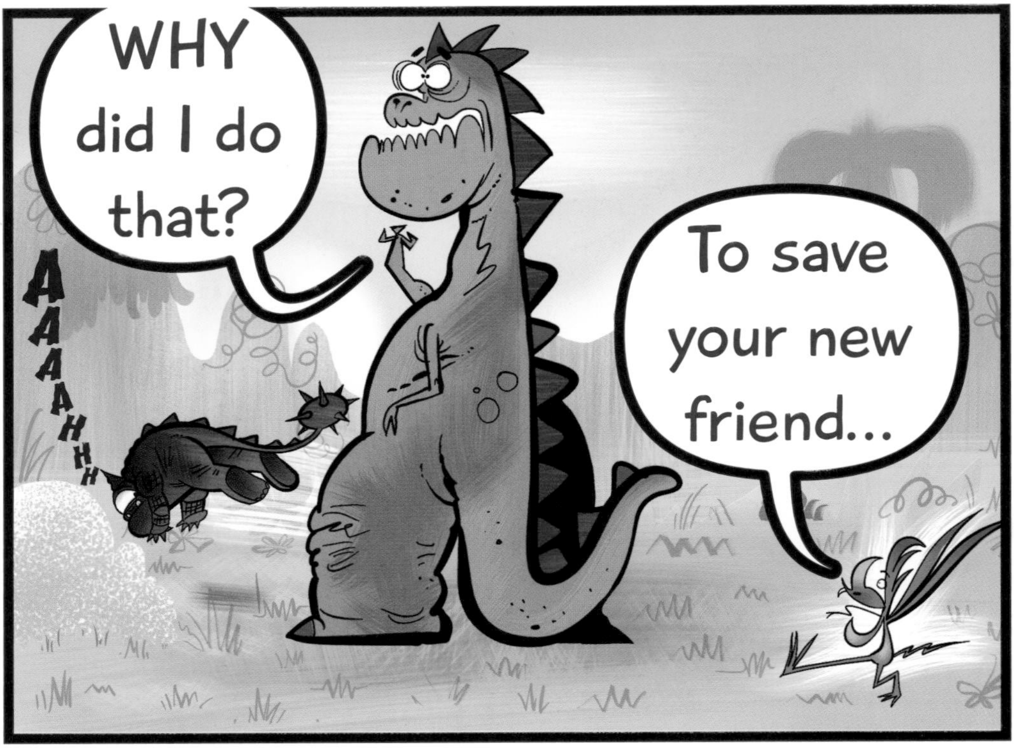
WHY did I do that?
AAAAAHHH
To save your new friend...

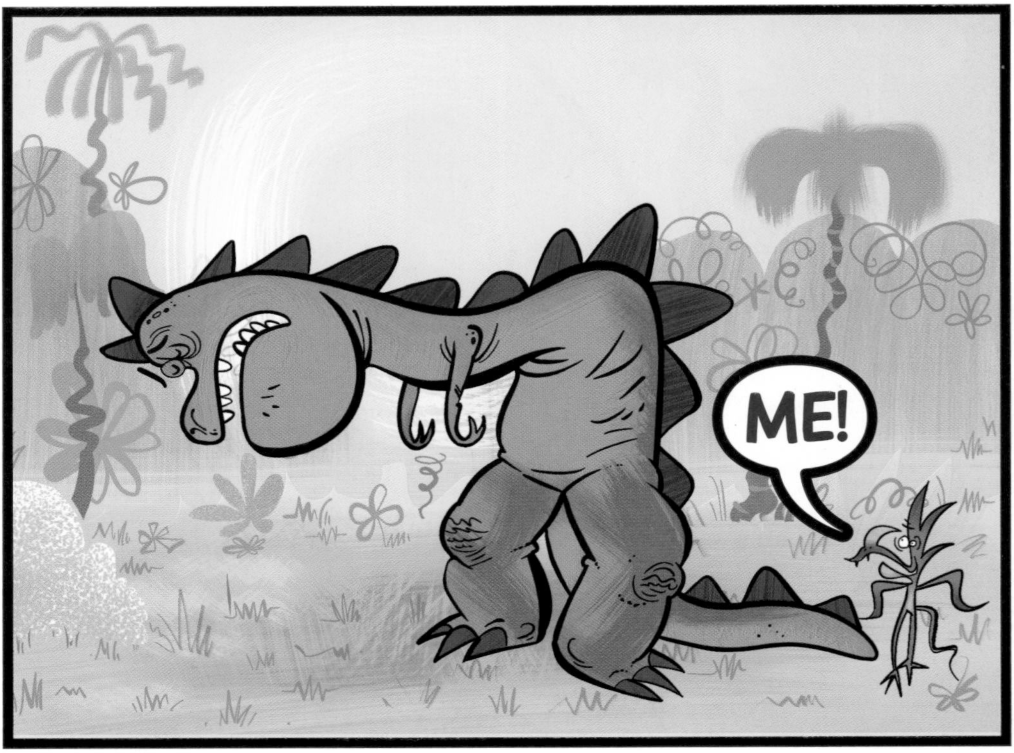
ME!

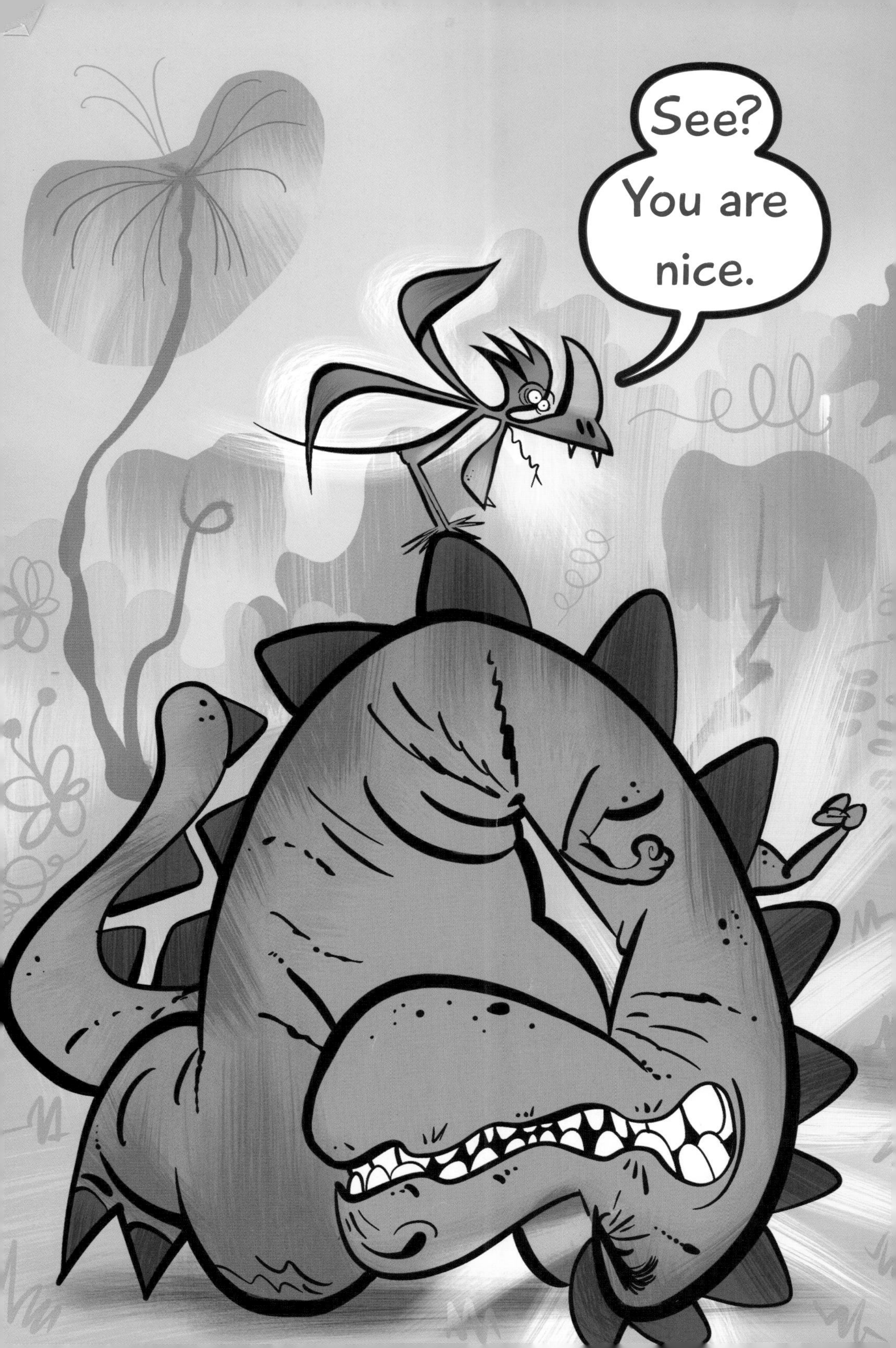
See? You are nice.

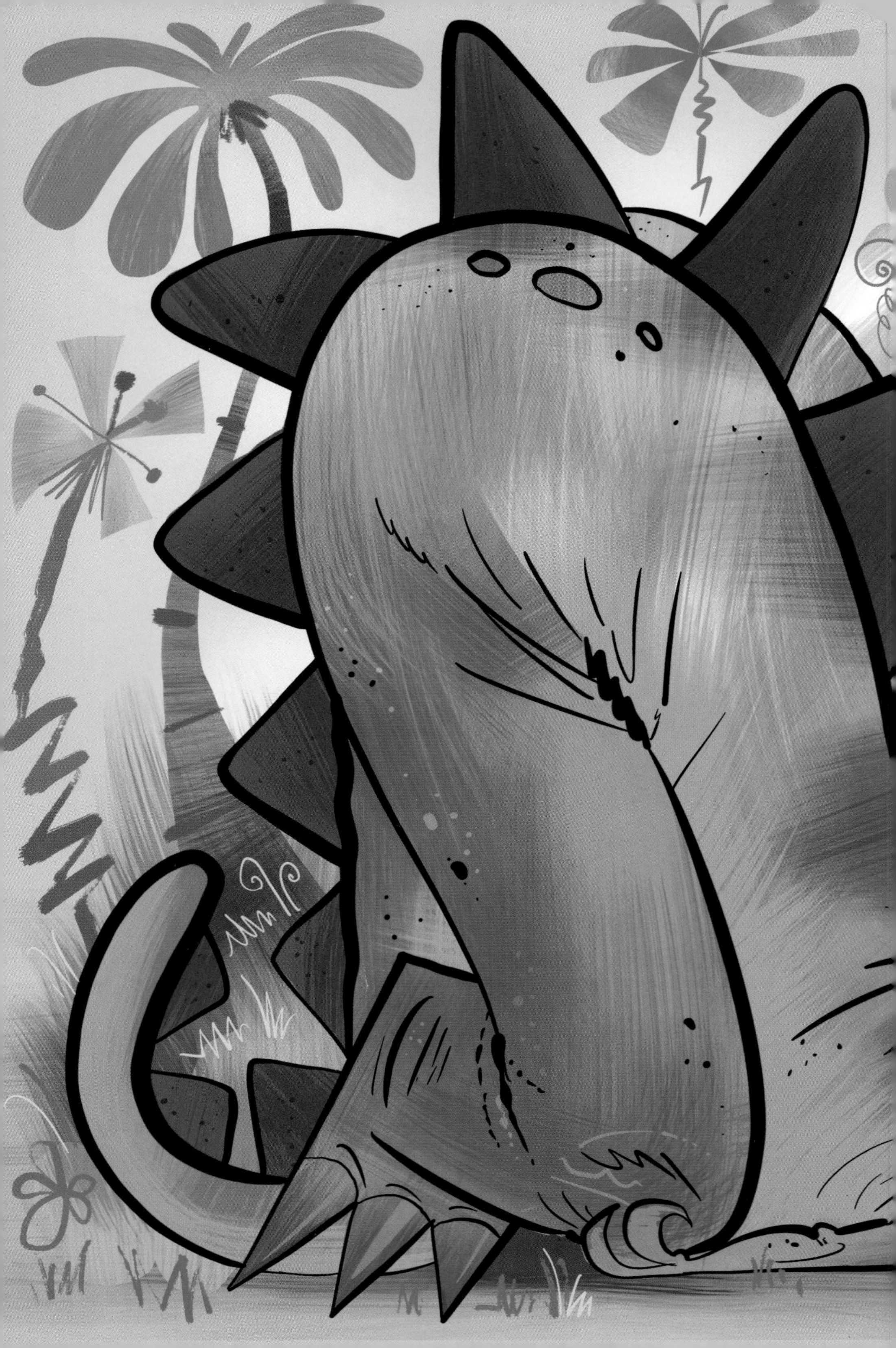

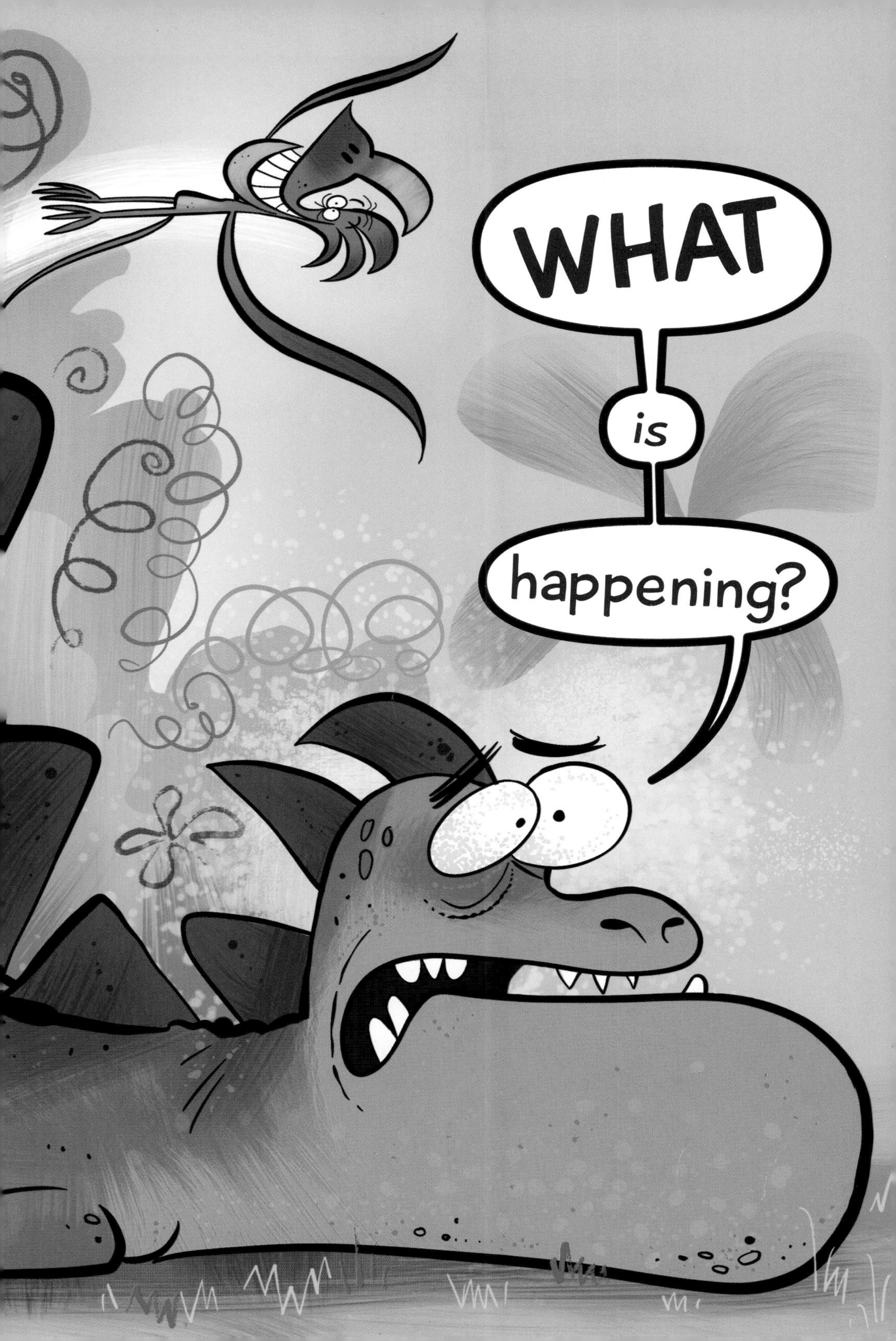
WHAT
is
happening?

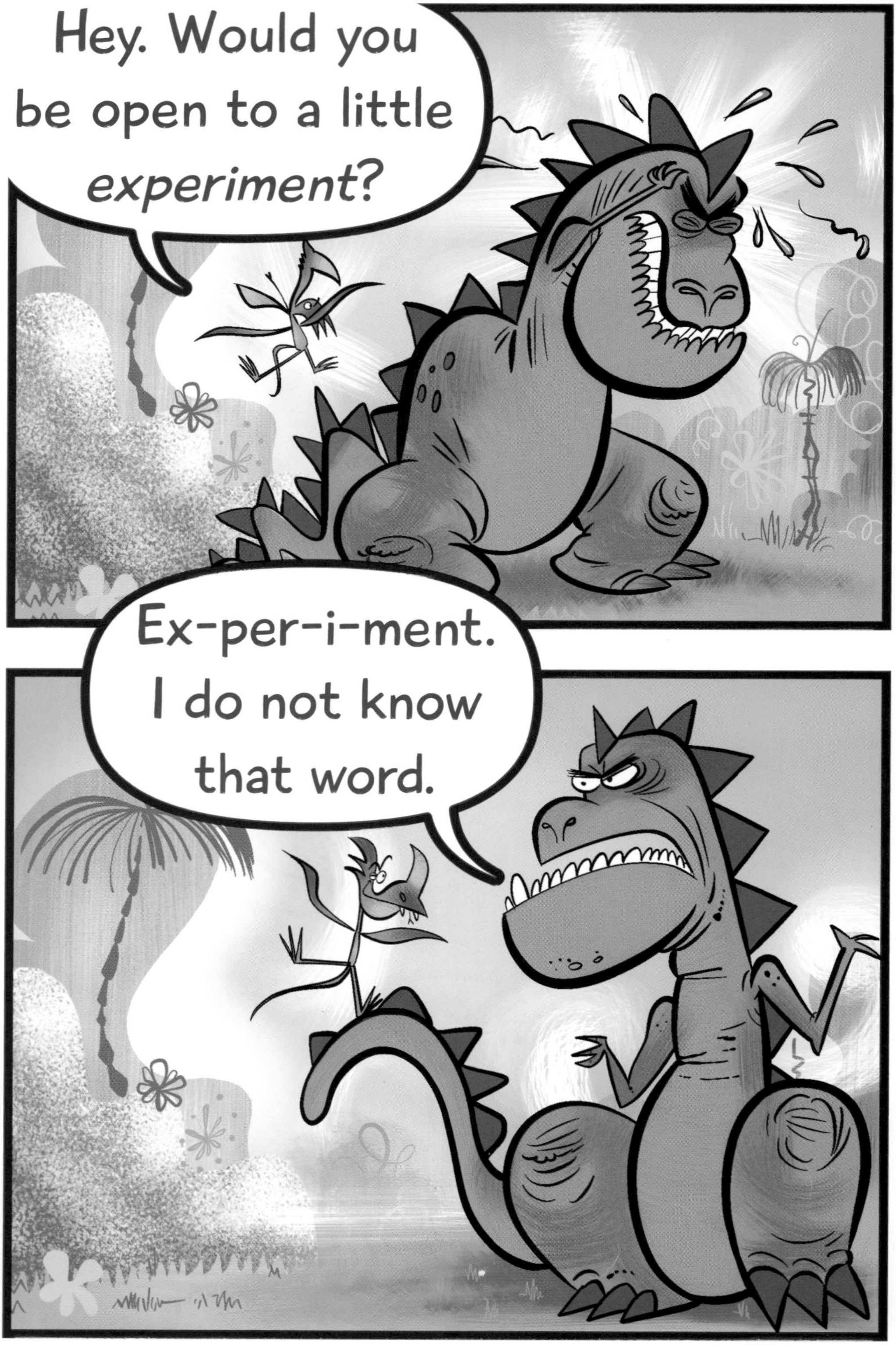
Hey. Would you be open to a little *experiment*?
Ex-per-i-ment. I do not know that word.

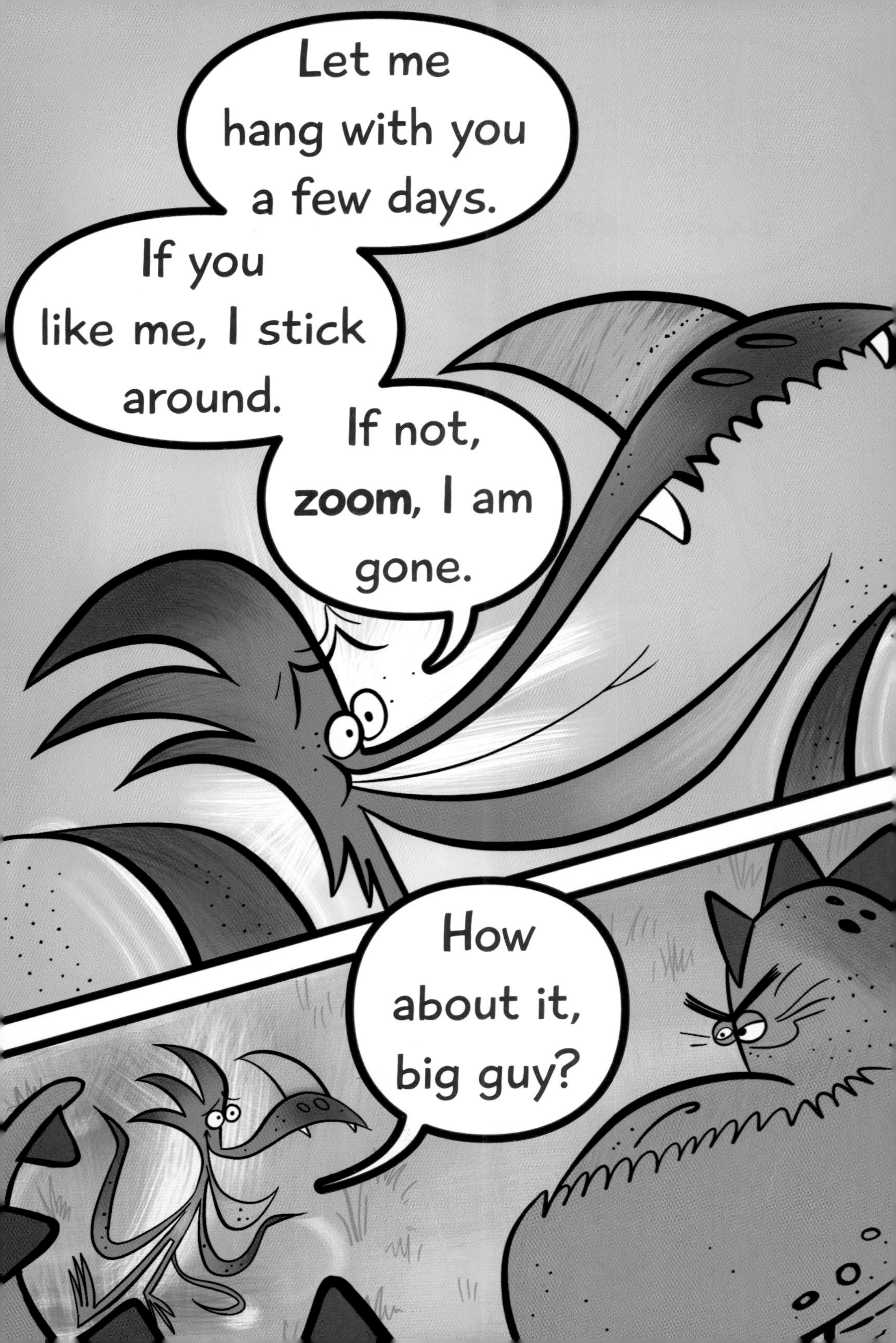
Let me hang with you a few days.
If you like me, I stick around.
If not, **zoom**, I am gone.
How about it, big guy?

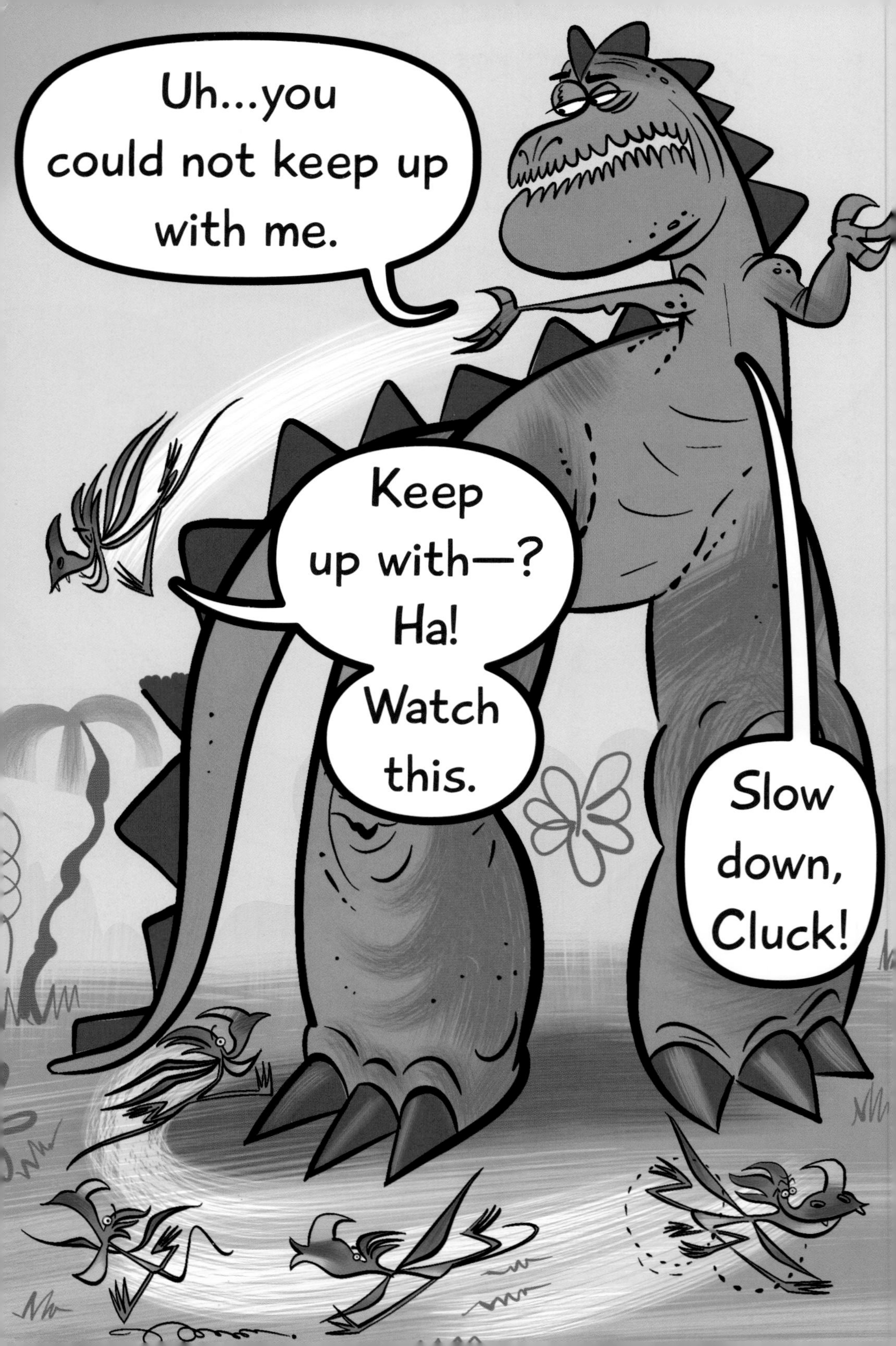
Uh...you could not keep up with me.
Keep up with—? Ha! Watch this.
Slow down, Cluck!

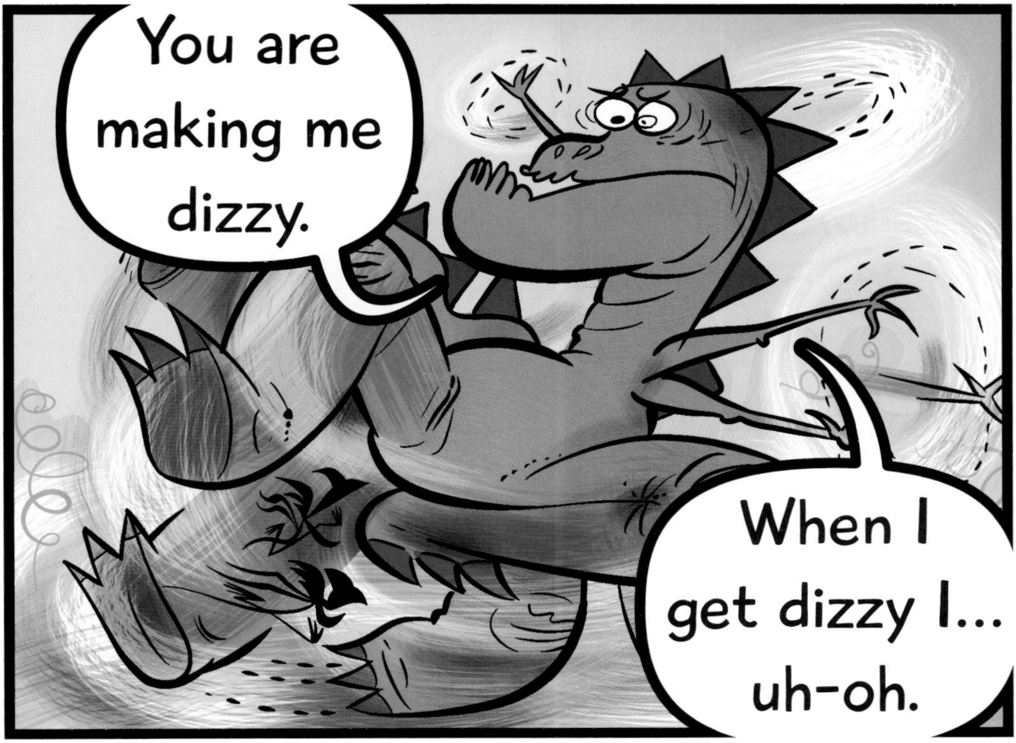
You are making me dizzy.
When I get dizzy I... uh-oh.

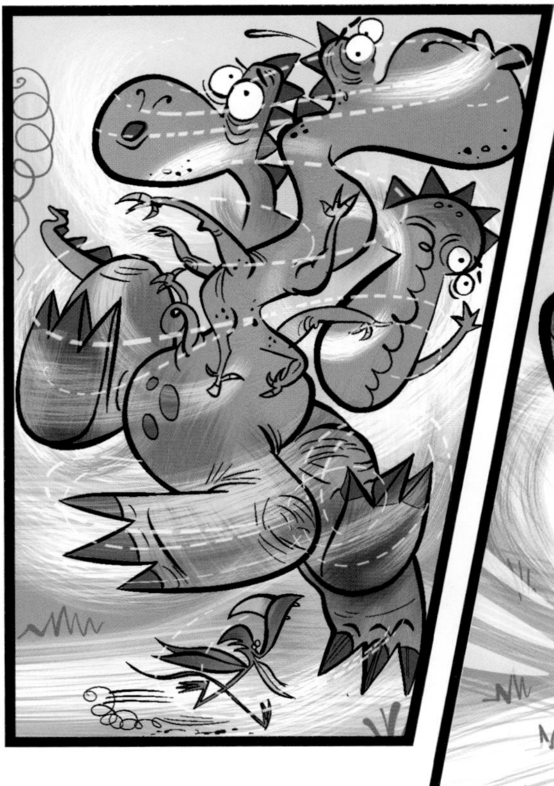

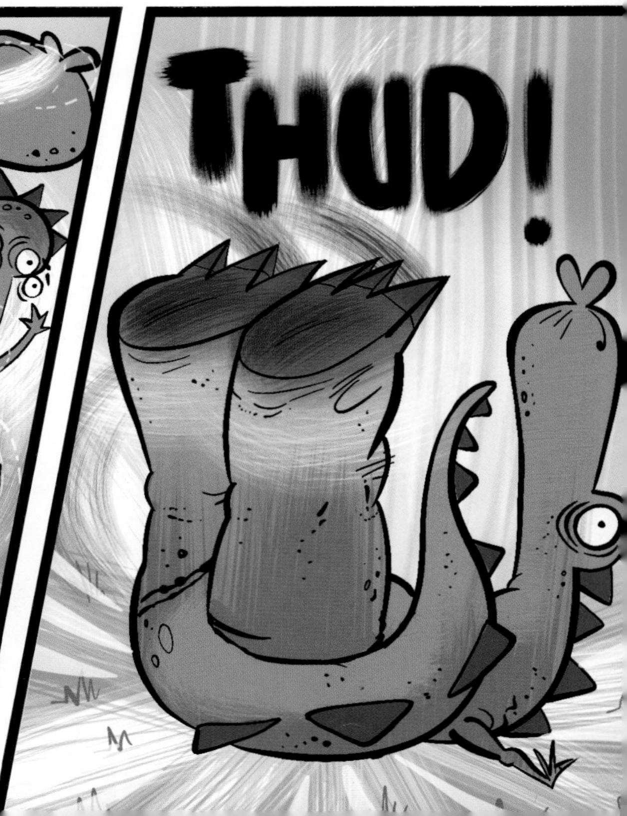
THUD!

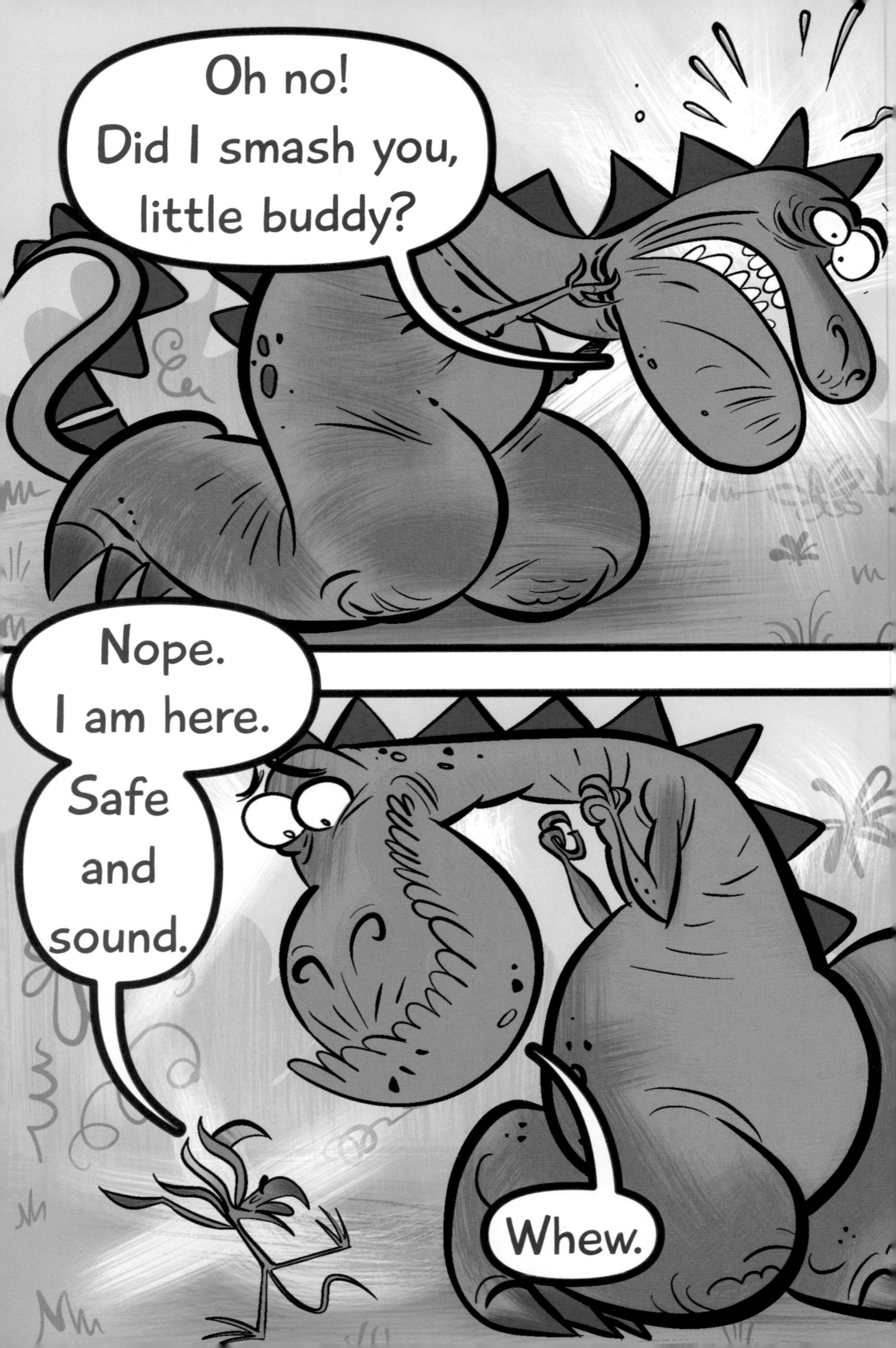
Oh no!
Did I smash you,
little buddy?
Nope.
I am here.
Safe
and
sound.
Whew.

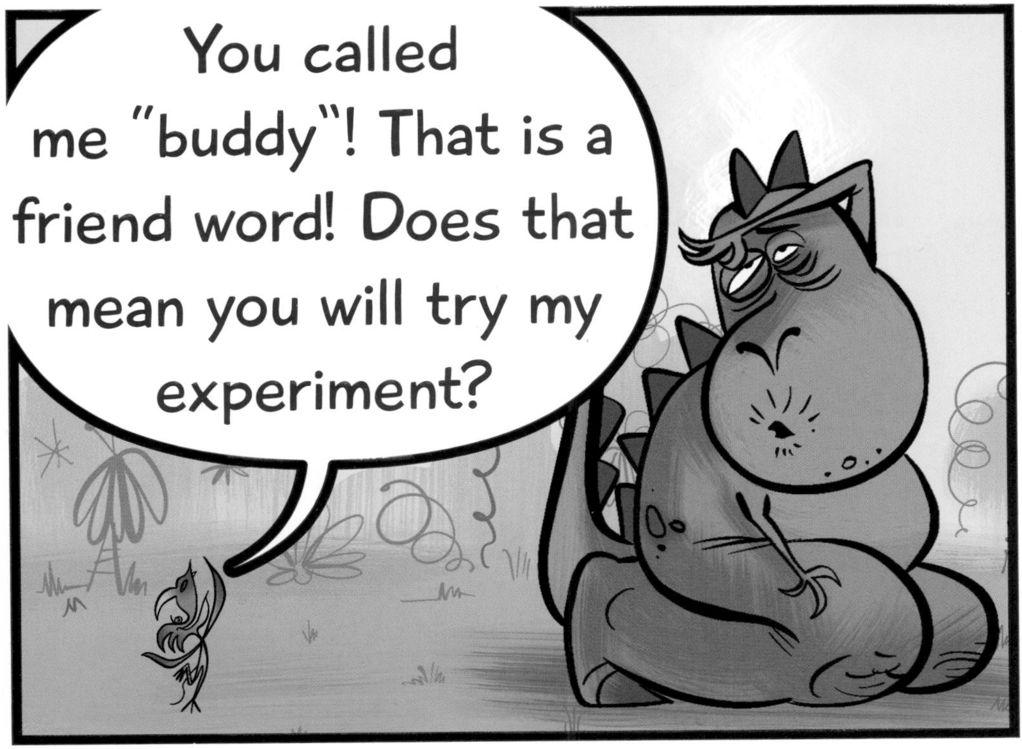
You called me "buddy"! That is a friend word! Does that mean you will try my experiment?

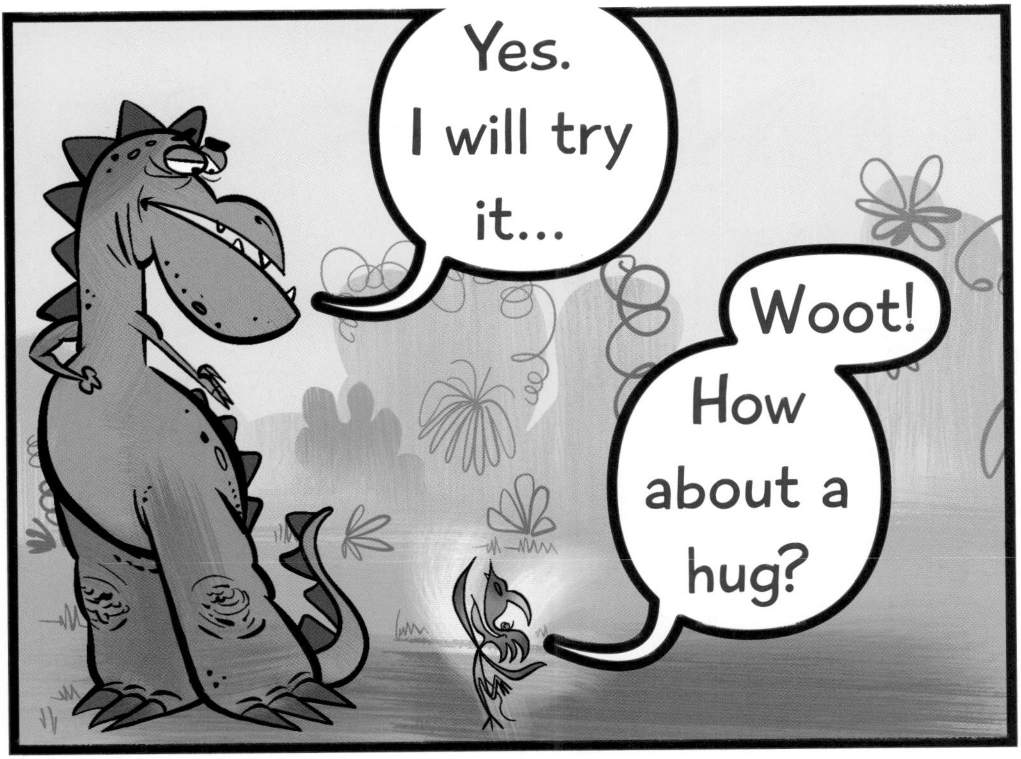
Yes. I will try it...
Woot!
How about a hug?

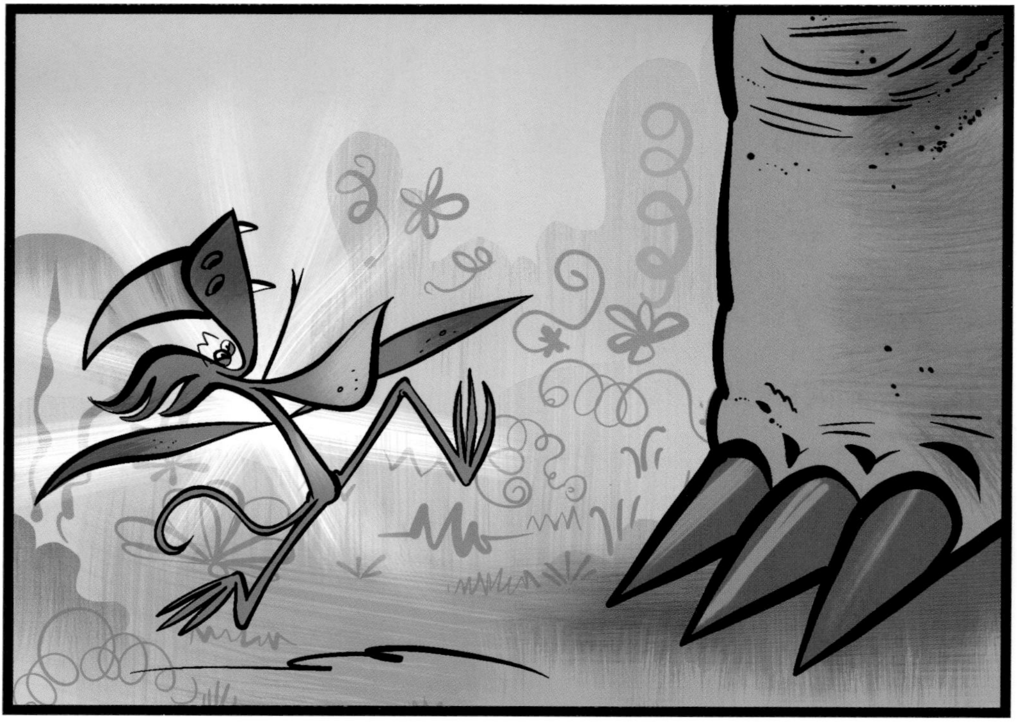
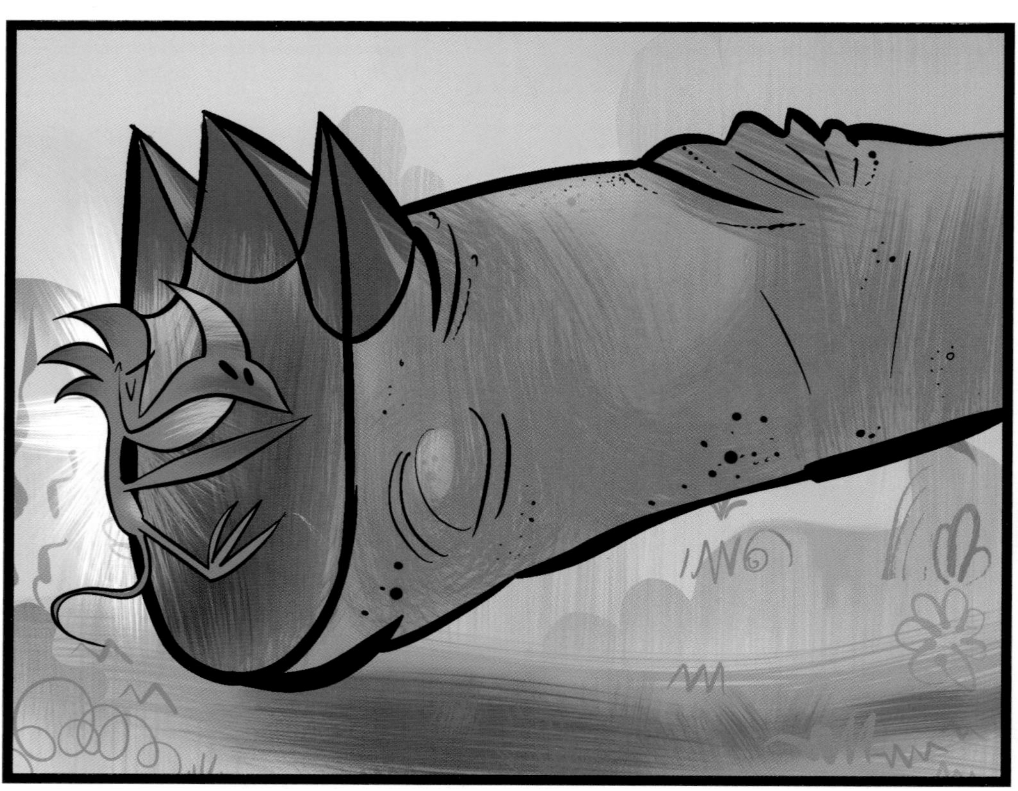

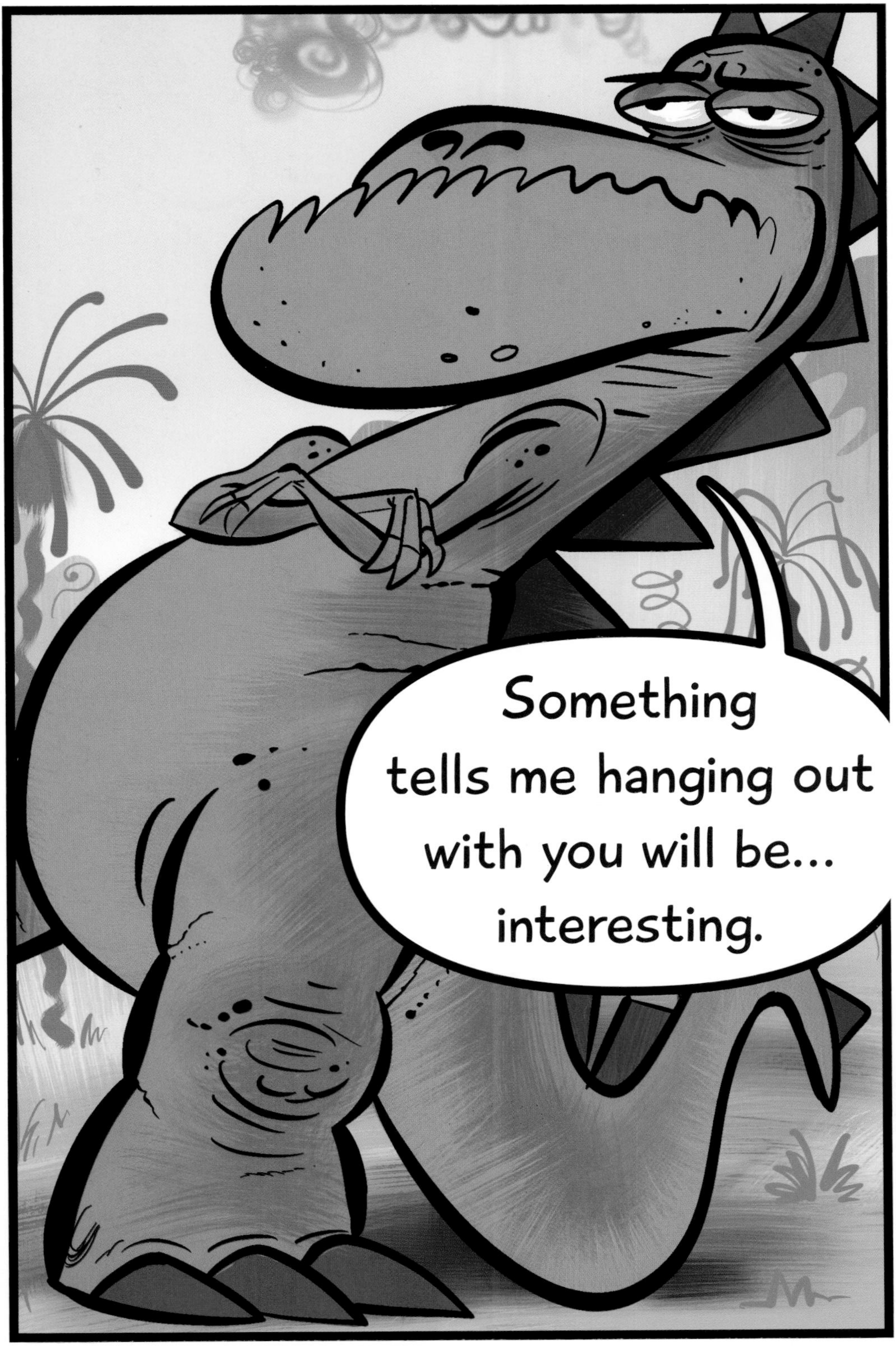
Something tells me hanging out with you will be... interesting.

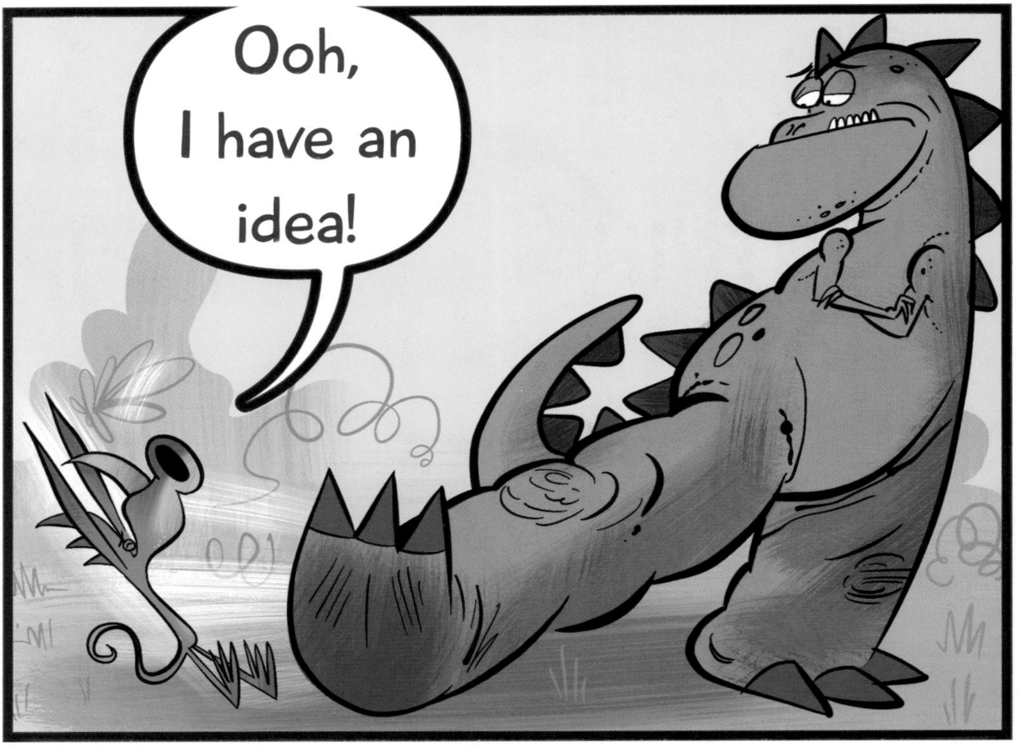
Ooh, I have an idea!

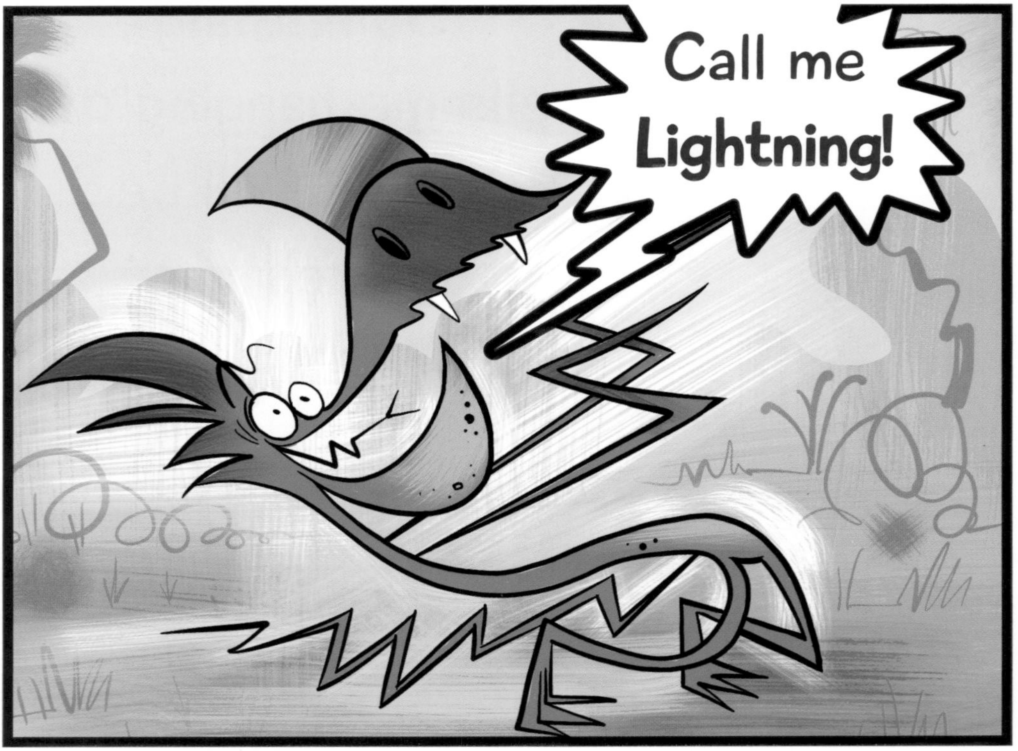
Call me **Lightning!**

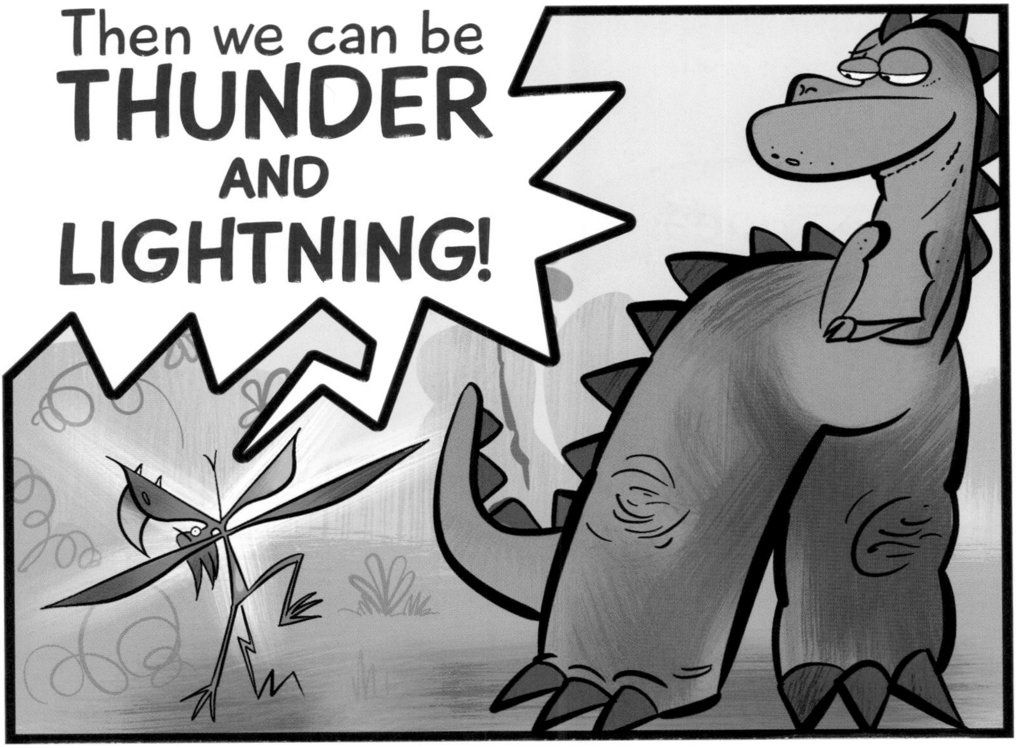
Then we can be THUNDER AND LIGHTNING!

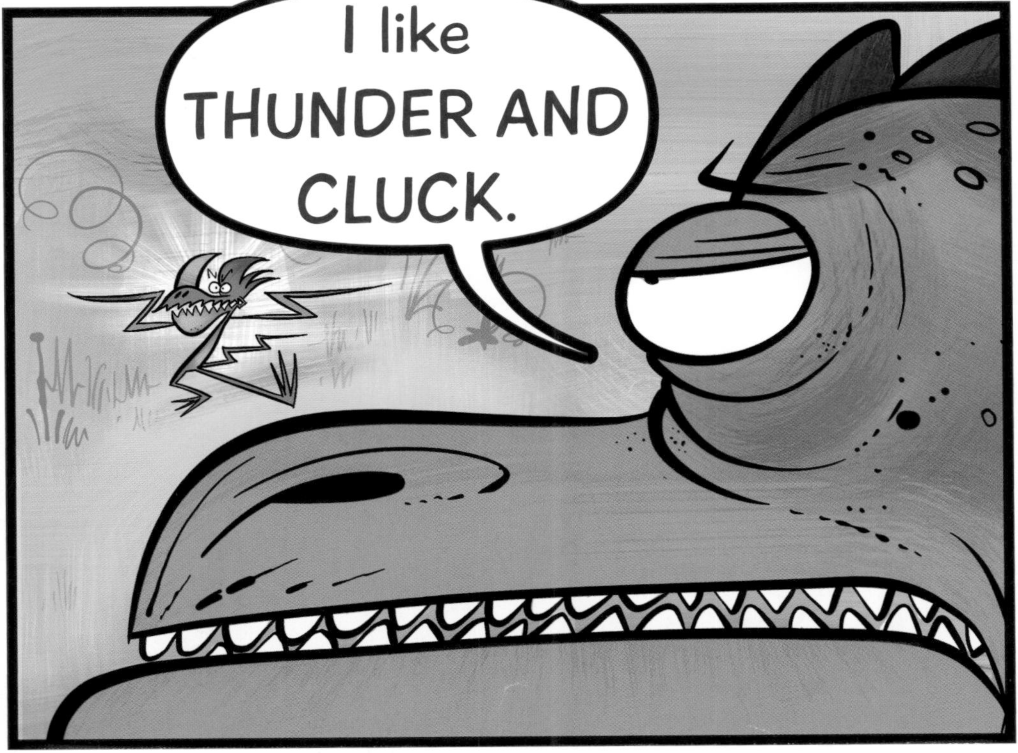
I like THUNDER AND CLUCK.

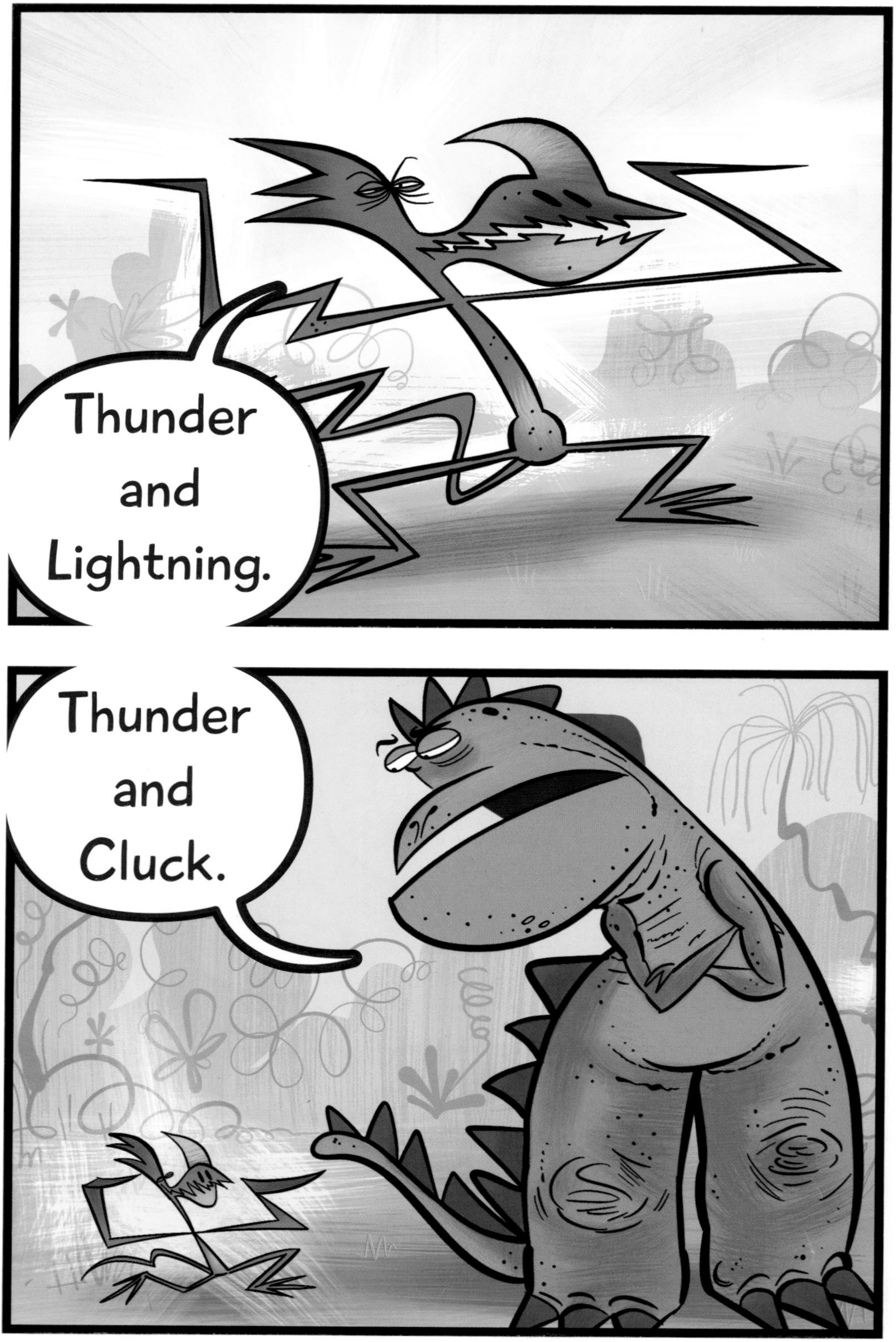
Thunder and Lightning.
Thunder and Cluck.

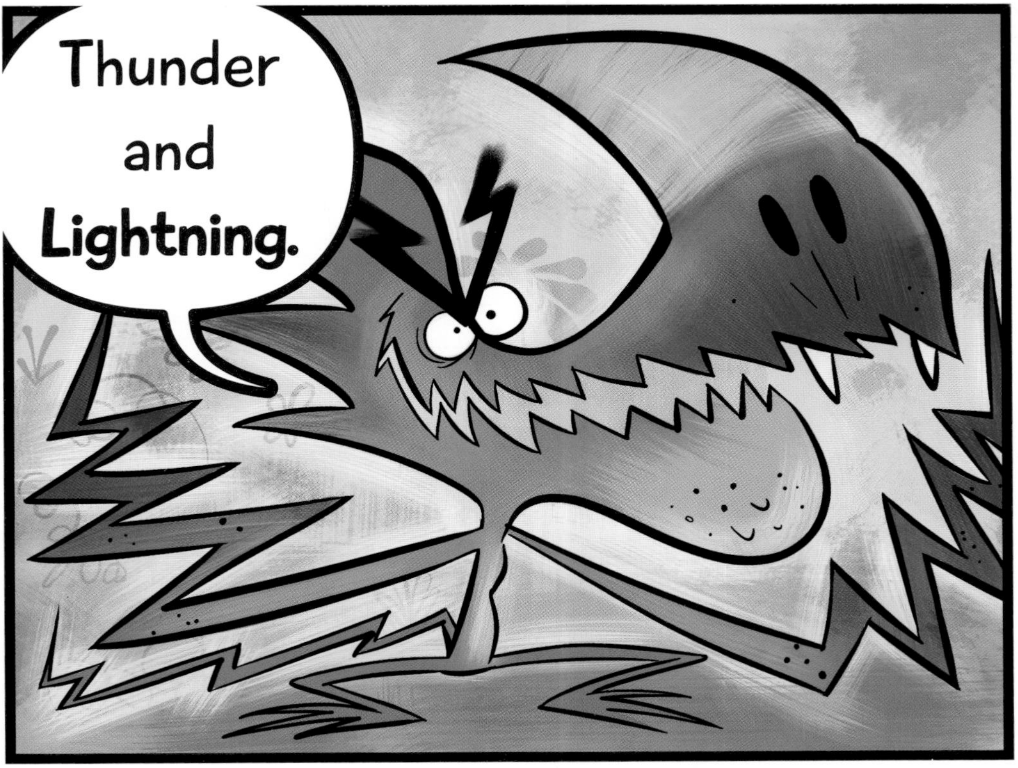
Thunder and **Lightning.**

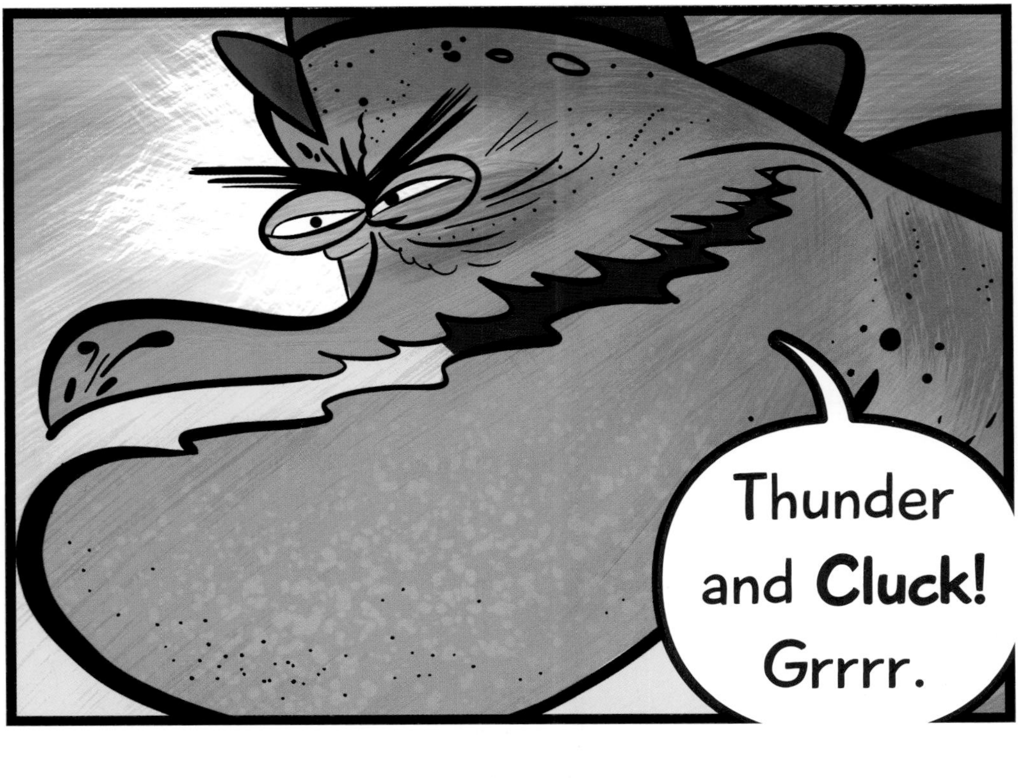
Thunder and **Cluck!** Grrrr.

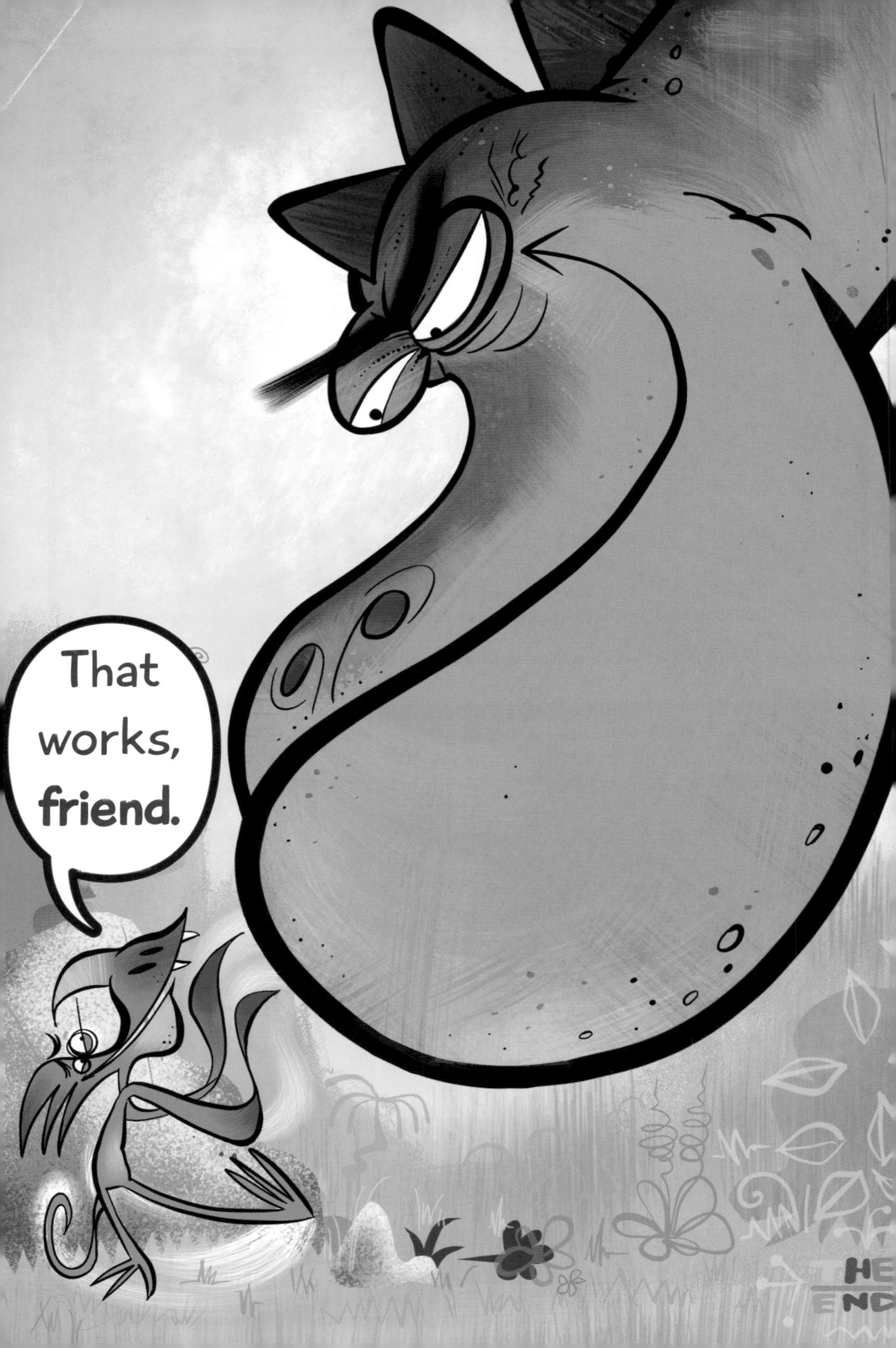
That works, friend.